EMOTIONALLY BROKEN

Isabel Wells

Emotionally Broken
Written By Isabel Wells

www.isabel-wells.com
Cover Art & Book Design by Rayah Jaymes

ISBN: 978-0-578-71496-7

DEDICATION

This book was written for all those women who are either in a relationship with a narcissist or going through the recovery phase of narcissistic abuse.

Ladies, I want to share this story of how easy it is to enter a toxic relationship and if you can understand what to look for, you can avoid the heartache in the future.

First, never ignore your gut feelings. Your gut and intuition will never steer you wrong. Secondly, don't settle just to be with someone; it's okay to be alone. And finally, look for someone who values you and who enhances your life and does not create drama and stress. Life is short. Why spend it with someone who doesn't treat you the way you should be treated? The one thing that is most valuable and that you can't get back is your time. Spend it with the people that make you happy.

So, for those who just left an abusive relationship, remember you are strong and you're a fighter and you will be okay. For those who are questioning the red flags don't. Move on because those small red flags become open fire on your heart and self-esteem when you let your guard down.

I am dedicating this book to my two boys. They are my world. I realized that to be able to make sure my world was safe and happy I needed to be the best version of myself free from stress and anxiety. Thanks to them, and to new beginnings, we are happy and enjoying life.

INTRODUCTION

WHEN I FIRST GOT MARRIED, I HAD NEVER HEARD about narcissism and what narcissistic abuse was all about. Narcissism has become a common mental health diagnosis. There are many YouTube videos, books, and blogs about narcissistic abuse so we can become educated on how to recognize the red flags.

For the purposes of this book, I reference the husband as the narcissist, but there are many female narcissists out there that cause the same emotional, verbal, and even physical abuse to their partner. There are many reasons why women and men decide to stay with their narcissistic, abusive partner. Maybe there are kids involved and she fears what her husband may do to the kids if he is alone with them. Maybe she doesn't have the self-esteem to think she deserves anything better.

Whatever the reason is, the reality is that narcissists all follow the same patterns and put their victims through the same stages of abuse when they enter a relationship. It's important to know the red flags early so you don't get trapped or invested in a toxic relationship that causes you harm. The phases begin when you first meet them with the love-bombing phase. The term means exactly how it sounds. They send an explosion of love your way through compliments, texts, gifts, and attention that makes you feel you have won the lottery and are so thankful. The belief that he is your soulmate becomes blinding like a spotlight in your eyes, and their true intentions are hidden in the shadows.

Once they have piqued your interest and you begin to invest your time, energy, and emotions in them, then you begin to experience the isolation phase. This is when they slowly instigate friction or isolation between you and your close friends and family. They start to express their disapproval and find fault with the ones you love. Slowly you distance yourself from family and friends, making them the only person left in your world. That isolation makes you a prime target for them to control and manipulate you.

At this point, he can easily bring you into the devaluing phase where he criticizes, puts you down, and makes you believe you're the problem because you lack the ability to communicate effectively. He gaslights you, making you think you're crazy and don't remember what was said or what happened correctly or even at all. He has taken his mask off and you now see the true colors of the narcissist, whose goal is to lower your self-esteem so much you don't think you are worth anything without him.

This phase is continuous and never ending, taking you to your breaking point and then making a 180-degree turn to a loving man who comes to the rescue. He uplifts you enough only to break you again. When a narcissist sees you crying and begging that's when they swoop in with kindness and flowers to make you feel like there is hope. Narcissists feel important this way, and this vicious cycle repeats endlessly unless you become strong enough to walk away.

Many people never get to the recovery phase, where they finally decided they can no longer live with a toxic partner and can pick up what dignity they have left and walk out. It is not easy speaking from my own experience of being married to a narcissist. You end up living life with the hope that it will get better if you try harder.

I am not a psychologist so I can only write about my experience with my ex-husband, but when I finally found out what I was dealing with, I began reading everything I could get my hands on about narcissists, and I went to a trained professional to help me get through the abuse. Understanding what I was dealing with and the reality that my situation would never change unless I had the power to change it for myself, gave me the willpower to walk away.

For all the individuals out there that are dealing with a toxic partner or family member, I hope this book can help you realize that there is hope and there is life after narcissistic abuse. Remember, you do not need to confine yourself to your situation or your toxic relationship. It's not easy to walk away. It's challenging and it's scary, but it's life changing. **You will survive and, in the end, you will be a stronger person.**

CHAPTER ONE

Putting Myself Out There

NO MORE. I WAS DONE GIVING HIM "ONE MORE" chance only to have it blow up in my face.

I checked my phone to make sure the GPS app wasn't on and changed all my passwords to anything that he could access. That morning I scheduled an appointment with a lawyer. Early. I sat in the parking lot of the lawyer's office in my car with my head in my hands for what felt like forever. The feeling of being lost consumed me. I didn't know whether to scream or cry. I straightened up, took a deep breath in, and let out a long, slow sigh. I flipped open my sun-visor mirror to check that my makeup was still intact, shook off my apprehension, and got out of my car. I walked through the doors of the law firm and took my first step of what I considered as the beginning of my journey to taking my life back. I headed over to the receptionist's desk, clutching my purse close to my chest. I found myself having to focus on walking as my mind was filled with conflicting thoughts about fear of leaving my husband versus the liberating feeling of no longer being abused.

Somehow, I actually made it to the receptionist's desk. She looked up at me, smiled, and held up her right index finger, signaling me to hold on. I stood there in silence, listening to the thump of my heart beating, which felt like it was coming out of my chest. I nervously chewed my fingernails.

"Good morning, may I help you?" asked the receptionist after hanging up the phone.

"Umm...hello, yes I have an appointment with Mrs. Dempsey. My name is Katelyn Price," I replied. My voice was quivering and I realized I was slouching, so I took a deep breath, straightened my shoulders, hoping to show some semblance of confidence in the reason I was here.

"Okay, dear, just have a seat in the lobby. Mrs. Dempsey will be right with you," she replied as she re-focused her attention back on her computer screen. The lobby was nicely decorated. There was a black leather sofa that I gravitated to and took a seat. I distracted myself by flipping through the various law magazines displayed on the coffee table. I had zero interest in the articles and my brain was in a fog; I couldn't focus on the articles even if I wanted to. I quietly flipped through the pictures with a blank gaze. The receptionist finally called me in, and I followed her with my shoulders slumped down and my body trembling. Mrs. Dempsey's office was beautifully furnished with a mahogany grand desk in the center of the room and two leather lounge chairs for her clients to sit in. There were matching bookcases on either side of her desk filled with hardcovers of what I could only assume were legal books. Behind her desk was a wall of windows that overlooked a small Chicago park. Mrs. Dempsey was an older lady with shoulder-length gray hair, and a warm smile that was very welcoming and put me at ease. She stood up to shake my hand.

"Hello. My name is Mrs. Dempsey. Don't be nervous, dear. Have a seat," She said. I had a million anxious thoughts going through my head and I couldn't trust my voice to provide a rational reply to her greeting. The best I could do was muster up a half smile as I took a seat in one of the leather chairs in front of her desk.

"Okay, Mrs. Price, let's begin. Let's start with something easy. What your current address is, is this the marital home, and are still living there?" she asked, getting ready to write in her blank file that she had labeled with my name.

"My address is 668 Oil Street, Chicago, Illinois, and yes, it is the marital home and I still live there with my two daughters, my husband, and my stepson," I replied with a trembling voice that cracked in between every word. I felt like I had a lump in my throat and could barely speak. Thankfully, Mrs. Dempsey noticed.

"Would you like a glass of water, Mrs. Price?" asked the lawyer. I nodded yes. She picked up her phone and called the receptionist. "Elizabeth, can you please bring Mrs. Price a bottle of water?"

The receptionist came right in with a cold bottle of water for me. My hands were shaking but reached for the bottle of water she brought for in for me. With just about zero grace, I clumsily managed to fumble open the plastic bottle and take a long drink to try to calm my nerves.

"A bit better, Mrs. Price?"

"Yes, I think so. Thank you," I replied.

"Good. Do you think you're ready to tell me your story?" Mrs. Dempsey asked, sitting upright, waiting to write down the information she needed for her file.

In my mind, when I'd prepared myself for this, when

I could finally share all that I had been going through in my courtship and marriage, I thought I'd be able to be in control of my emotions. Instead, I broke down sobbing, then slowly, I began to talk.

"I want a divorce. I can no longer handle living with my husband. I have endured his emotional and verbal abuse for five years and I need out," I said with a choppy voice. Then I continued to tell her my story.

"Okay, Mrs. Price. Thank you for sharing all that with me. I know it was difficult for you. Let me get the paperwork started, and I'll need a retainer before you leave. Get some rest, you have had a stressful day," said Mrs. Dempsey.

I wrote her a check, thanked her as we shook hands, and then I left the office. I quickly dashed back to my car. As I sat inside, feeling embarrassed for breaking down in the office, I also felt ashamed. I realized I no longer was that strong, independent woman I was when living in Detroit and first met Jonathan Price. Instead, I'd become a codependent, hot mess of a lady who was controlled, shamed, and mistreated. How could I have accepted such abuse for so many years, causing me to lose my self-confidence? Could I possibly feel any worse about myself and my situation? How did I end up in a lawyer's office crying after falling in love and marrying the person I thought was my fairy-tale prince charming?

It all started about five years ago. I was working and taking care of my kids living in Detroit, Michigan as a single mother. It wasn't easy doing it all by myself. My days would start at 5:30 in the morning, and I didn't stop until my kids went to bed. Most days I survived purely on caffeine. Every morning, my mother would hear my alarm, and as I was getting ready, she would go downstairs to the kitchen to brew me a pot of coffee. It was our daily routine.

"Good morning, Ma," I would say as I ran down the stairs, zipping up my jeans and buckling my belt in a rush. I had the tendency to hit the snooze button far too many times until I had no time left to do anything at a normal human pace.

"Morning, Kate. When will you be home tonight?" replied my mom while handing me a thermos of coffee and the lunch bag I had prepared the night before fully knowing I wouldn't have time in the morning.

"Thanks, Ma, see you tonight around six," I yelled behind me as I grabbed my purse and keys and dashed out the door.

"Have a good day, Kate," I heard my mother holler back before the door closed behind me.

I was truly fortunate my mom was retired and was able to stay home with my daughters, so I didn't have to take them to daycare. I had the girls when I was in my early twenties, and my marriage didn't last more than a year. We got married as soon as I was pregnant with Hailey, and we had Sofia the year after. The girls' father disappeared shortly after Sofia was born to pursue his career. I was left to raise our two babies all by myself with no job. I didn't have a choice but to move in with my mom so I could go to work. I found a job at a steel mill in Detroit. I made a decent wage, which was enough to pay for food and utilities but not enough for daycare. The hours were long, but it paid the bills. The factory was loud and dirty. I would sweat just breathing. Most of the day my face would be an unflattering shade of beet red, and by the time my shift ended, my clothes were drenched in sweat.

We all lived in a tiny 950-square-foot three-bedroom house. We were all crammed in with my mother as we tried to make ends meet. The girls shared the one bedroom and my mom and I each had our own. The fridge was never full. We lived on the basics. We ate spaghetti most nights with butter or pasta sauce. I struggled for birthday gifts for the girls, and Christmas was especially hard for me. A mom was supposed to be able to spoil her kids, and I never had enough to be able to do that. The neighborhood we lived in was old, with gang graffiti on most of the convenience stores, street signs, and bridges. I grew up in this neighborhood and knew it well. It wasn't great, but I couldn't afford my own place on my salary. My days were nothing to brag about. They consisted of going to work during the day and coming home to the girls at night. There was no room to do anything else for me. Most days I was stuck working overtime and I would pull into the driveway after dinner. My mom would feed the girls for me and then send me a million texts making sure I was still alive if I wasn't home by dinner.

"Kate, where are you?"

"Are you still at work?"

"Are you okay?"

"Why aren't you home yet? Dinner is ready."

"How much longer before you get here? The girls are asking for you."

"Kate?"

These were typical texts my mom would send if I had to work overtime.

"Mom, I will be home later; I'm working late again."

"Stop bombarding my phone with texts please."

"I'm safe," I would text back. I knew I didn't work in a good area, but my mom was sometimes overprotective, which drove me crazy. She acted like I was still ten years old and needed to know where I was all the time, or else she would release a search and rescue team.

When I did get home, I would take a shower to get off all the dirty sweat, and then the evening was spent with Sofia and Hailey. We were all crammed in a small house, but we had fun. I didn't have much energy when I got home, but what I did have would be used playing catch or having tea parties with the girls and their dolls. Every night we would snuggle up on the couch, make popcorn, and watch a show of their choice. I didn't have much of a social life; board games, parks, and cartoon-movie nights were my nightly entertainment. I didn't go shopping for clothes; I didn't do ladies' nights out or hair salon appointments, and I especially did not do the dating thing. Who had time for any of that?

Everything changed the day our company brought in an executive manager from our corporate office in Chicago to help with production. We were emailed about the purpose of his trip the week before he arrived.

Attention: Staff of DW Steel Mill Inc–Detroit Facility

From: Corporate Office

Subject: Continuous Improvement Initiative

As you may be aware, production has been suffering due to the downtime of our equipment. We need to provide the best quality and timing for our customer excellence program. We are bringing in one of our top senior managers from corporate to the facility to assist with various production techniques to optimize production. We are hopeful that you will welcome Jonathan Price to the facility. Jonathan will be working on our continuous improvement initiatives to bring significant changes to our process, improving our competitive advantage within the market. He will be approaching many of you to gain some history and knowledge of the process. Please support Mr. Price with his requests.

If you have any questions or concerns, please contact your shop manager.

Sincerely,

David West

CEO of DW Steel Mill Inc.

The following week, I saw Mr. Price on a tour of the mill with David West. He looked to be in his early forties, clean-shaven, and was dressed business casual. He was handsome and distinguished with salt and pepper hair. He had the bluest eyes that would make even the Caribbean Sea look pale. As people approached him, he smiled, shook their hands, and made eye contact. He took the time to learn their names, and he seemed interested in every person who talked to him. When he smiled, I could almost feel warmth emanating from him. He seemed polite and charming, and he had a confidence about him that was very attractive. Of course, this was my view of him from afar. His signature dress code on the factory floor consisted of gray dress pants with sharp, defining creases down the front and back and an all-white well-pressed dress shirt with equivalent creases along the sides of his sleeves. I could tell by the muscles rippling underneath his shirt that he worked out during his spare time. If his trousers were just a bit tighter, they would have shown off his ass. I guessed it was a bitable one, but his slacks weren't that tight. That combination on him made him look important, and his presence demanded respect. He smelled clean when he walked past me, and his cologne smelled so masculine and enhanced his attractiveness.

I hadn't had naughty thoughts like this since I was a high-school teenager. I needed to stop that. I couldn't be giving him the *come here so I can bite you* look. People would start to notice; he would notice. I was extremely taken by him, but he was totally out of my league. He was obviously smarter than me by his position in the company he held; plus, he was dressed like a high-class professional, and he was just so beautiful. But it didn't matter because I didn't date guys from work. Although it wasn't company policy, it was a rule I used as an excuse to keep guys away if they asked me out. I wasn't doing the dating thing, but I never said anything about not admiring from a distance. What was the harm in window-shopping, right?

I didn't think he had even noticed me when I first saw him because he was always either surrounded by leadership or on the go. And what was there to notice? I was a twenty-seven-year-old working-class lady, and I was always dressed like one of the guys. Dirty, ripped jeans; the company shirt; and my long, wavy, black hair tied up in a messy bun to make sure it was clear of any running machinery. I couldn't wear jewelry of any type, but I always made sure I wore bright red lipstick. One thing my mama taught me was to never leave the house without lipstick. Heck, it was almost the first thing I would put on after my bra and underwear in the morning!

Every day we would have a daily morning wrap-up meeting at work about the previous day's challenges and output. I always took meeting minutes, never paying attention to my surroundings as I scrambled to get everything written down on paper. One morning I looked up because I felt the burning feeling of eyes on me. It was Jonathan. He had been gazing at me with his intense blue eyes. He realized I noticed and instantly turned red and quickly looked away. At first glance, I could see a hint of a sexy smile when he blushed. I was sure he wasn't gazing at me sexually because there was nothing sexual about me when I was at work. He was probably daydreaming about someone back home, waiting for his morning coffee to kick in. Even though his daydreams weren't about me, it still made my heart skip a beat. I could feel the butterflies in my stomach suddenly waking up. I thought they were dead all these years. It had been so long–at least two or three years since I had had any feelings for a man, I had almost forgotten what it felt like. Of course, why did it have to be this guy I was attracted to? I apparently had good taste but let's be real. No man who had a prestigious career, success, and talent could possibly have eyes for a factory worker that wasn't going anywhere in life. I was never going to be one of those classy, successful, career-driven ladies that wore skinny pencil skirts, three-inch heels, and carried a leather briefcase to work. He is going to want a professional lady to be his partner in life, not someone like me.

Not that Jonathan felt attracted to me, but the idea that a "Jonathan type" could one day fall for me made me realize I wasn't just a mom; I was both a mom and a woman. I had forgotten that all these years. I only saw myself as a working mom, but I realized that I missed a man's attention. Maybe it was time I started dating again. I hadn't put myself out there in so long, I didn't even know how to date. I began twirling my hair, thinking about what it felt like again to have my knees become jelly from a first kiss or the butterflies in my stomach from a new relationship. Getting dressed up to go on a date or the anticipation of the first time in bed together. I didn't think I was ready for that again, and I certainly had no time for it. I had to focus on the girls; they were my priority. I quickly erased the ideas out of my head. *Back to work, Kate. This is your livelihood. Can't mess with it.*

Over the next couple weeks, I saw Jonathan occasionally and I couldn't get him out of my mind. I had a stupid schoolgirl crush. Knowing I couldn't have him for some reason made him more attractive and irresistible. It was an infatuation I had, and my mind began to play tricks on me. I began to have suspicions that he was sneaking glances back at me. At first, I thought he was just looking at something that was in the same direction as I was standing in, but it became more frequent, and he had a sexy undressing-me type of look about him. He would squint his eyes and lick his lips while locking his eyes on me. It was very sexy. I could feel his eyes move from my breasts to my hips and back up again. I tried to ignore him as I continued what I was working on, but it was incredibly hard. I found myself occasionally glancing back toward him. I am sure my outward looks were showing how eager I was to be in his arms and taste his lips. Every glance I would catch gave me a new shiver that would surge through my body. I liked it. I liked it a lot.

This man must be amazing in bed if he can give me this type of sensation with just a look, I thought.

Why did he have such a crazy effect on me? Was this pure attraction, chemistry, love at first sight–if such a thing even existed? I didn't really know. He wasn't the typical man I was attracted to. I was usually interested in tall, dark, European-looking men if I was even looking at all. He really wasn't very tall, and he certainly didn't have a European complexion. But there was something about him, and we kept locking eyes every time we would see each other. It was exhilarating and exciting. I became aware that I was looking forward to going to work in the mornings knowing I would get to see that tall drink of water. Who was I kidding though? What man would like someone with so much baggage like me? A woman who still lived at home with her mother and her two young kids. Especially this white-collar, elegant man who had so much going for himself.

Forget it, Kate.

I was dreaming up a fantasy that would never happen. I had no time for this nonsense.

Get back to work, I scolded myself.

It was a typical busy day at work. As a group leader in a steel factory, I oversaw the operators on the line, created daily reports on production, and worked alongside the maintenance crew to make sure the equipment was functional. Our meeting ran overtime into the lunch hour that day. I raced down the stairs from the engineering offices to the factory floor and headed to the lunchroom. As I made my way down the stairs, I realized Mr. Price was coming up. He stopped dead in his tracks, and I gasped for air as I realized he appeared to want to talk.

"Hello, my name is Jonathan Price," he said as he held his hand out for a handshake.

"Hi," I whispered shyly, holding out my hand for him to shake. "My name is Katelyn, um...Kate. Nice to meet you," I replied, trying not to stumble excessively over my own words. My knees were trembling, my heart was beating so fast it felt like it was going to jump out of my chest, and my gut felt like a butterfly emporium. I was on an emotional high, and I quickly became aware of my sweaty, shaking hand and snatched it back from our grip so he wouldn't notice. If he did notice, he didn't seem to react when I pulled away, but he did continue to stare into my eyes, smiling from ear to ear. I didn't know if I should stay and try to muster up enough nerves to continue a conversation or keep going and wish him well. But he didn't waste any time, and with his chest pushed outward and with a deep voice of confidence, he asked, "Have you eaten lunch yet, Kate? Because I would really like it if you could join me."

I froze and couldn't speak. My brain and my mouth became disconnected, and I was unable to form a coherent sentence, but I was able to hold it together enough to nod yes.

"Great, let's go. My car is right outside."

We walked together side by side. I kept my head down feeling the awkward silence, occasionally looking up at him and smiling politely. He pointed to his car, which was parked in one of the managers' reserved parking spaces the company allocated only for executives.

"I'm right there, the black Cadillac."

"Nice car," I replied as I gazed over the luxury sedan.

He drove a black CTS. It had the most beautiful paint job I had ever seen. The high-quality metallic black paint dazzled in the light and sparkled like a solitaire diamond. Jonathan walked alongside me to his car, making sure to open the passenger door for me. He was a gentleman; he was one of the few men that I could tell from people-watching that still practiced old-fashioned chivalry. He extended his hand out to help me into the passenger seat of his car. I felt like such a lady despite the fact I was wearing ripped-up jeans, construction boots, and had lines around my nose imprinted from the safety glasses we were required to wear all day.

His CTS was black on black, with beautiful graphite accents throughout. It felt so high class, especially compared to my little black Pontiac Sunfire I drove with cloth seats and cheap plastic trim throughout the interior. Without blinking, I intently watched him walk around to the driver's side, forgetting to swallow. I anxiously drummed my fingers against my lips as

I frantically tried to think of conversation topics to talk about when he got into the car. He clearly was a college-educated man because of the executive position he held at the company. He was well spoken, had a vocabulary that was unquestionably larger than mine, was confident, and had an attractive style that drew attention to him. I was none of those things. I was a high-school graduate with no college education, zero intellectual conversation, and limited self-confidence. What could we possibly have in common to talk about? The drive to the restaurant remained awkward with both of us feeling shy and timid, and I had the added feeling of nerves and total panic that I didn't want to make a fool of myself and say something stupid.

CHAPTER TWO
Mr. Right

WE WENT TO A LOCAL SANDWICH SHOP THAT was about a five-minute drive away from the factory but had a cute sitting area that was bistro style. It was a short drive, but I was able to calm my nervousness down enough to have a conversation by the time we arrived. We sat across from each other during lunch. I tried to keep my cool, but under the table I was fidgeting with my napkin on my lap as we chatted. Jonathan, on the other hand, stared intently, almost studying my every move. My tendency to stutter or draw a blank when I got too nervous was a given, so avoiding eye contact or staring down at the napkin I was playing with helped me maintain my composure.

"So, Kate, how long have you worked at the mill?" he asked.

"Oh, for a long time, at least four or five years, maybe longer–it has been so long, I've lost count," I replied with a slight nervous laughter. I was having a brain fart and felt like an idiot not even knowing how long I had worked at the steel mill.

“Umm… How about you? How long have you worked for corporate?” I replied, having no idea what else to ask him and wanting to steer the conversation back to him. I felt embarrassed about my unimpressive, simple answer.

“Not too long. I just started a couple months ago. It was a lateral move. I thought it would be good for my career. My next move will be vice president. This is a good steppingstone toward that goal,” he replied. *Great, I am with the next vice president and he is accompanied by a dull blue-collar worker. This isn’t going to end well for me*, I thought to myself as I consciously analyzed the possible outcome of our lunch together.

Jonathan then again bounced the conversation back to me. “Do you have any children?” Our conversation was like a game of tennis, with each one of us constantly trying to get rid of the conversation ball.

“I have two beautiful little girls, Hailey and Sofia. They are only three and four years old. They are both super chatty and hyper and they live with me. My ex-husband left when they were babies and I have raised them by myself,” I answered. “What about you, do you have any kids?” I asked, trying not to dominate the conversation. I had a habit of excessively talking out of nervousness, and I didn’t want to expose too much of myself too early. The less I told him right away the better. I didn’t want to risk scaring him off. If I told him I hadn’t gone to college and that I was still living with my mother, he would have run for the hills.

“I have one son, Scott. He is fifteen years old. He is an introvert. He lives with his mother most of the time, which I don’t understand because I have a six-bedroom house and she’s in a two-bedroom apartment. Where is the logic in that?” He sounded unimpressed and irritated about the circumstances of his relationship with his son and his ex-wife.

"It sounds like this is a sensitive topic," I replied, feeling his mood shift and realizing that I needed to change the subject soon.

"It is. My ex-wife is no help with keeping Scott on track at school, yet she insists on him staying with her. Scott is smart, but she isn't pushing him in school and the result is he is getting poor grades. It's her fault and I think I am a far better influence for Scott. Unfortunately, it's his choice, and I am not home enough to push the matter in court," he replied without hesitation, almost as if he had just had a recent conversation with his ex-wife about that very topic.

As we continued to talk, I realized we had almost nothing in common other than we both were recently divorced, but the attraction was still there, and I could feel the chemistry between us. We finished lunch, headed back to work, and parted ways for the rest of the day.

That evening I went home and thought about our lunch. Or was it a date? I couldn't get Jonathan Price out of my mind. I kept replaying our lunch over and over in my head, and every time my infatuation of him grew. But I needed to get a grip. There was no way an executive manager who had so much to offer would be interested in a nobody like me. We are completely different in every way. He was just being friendly. He didn't even give me a hug when we came back from lunch, and not once did he reached for my hand or anything that would suggest he was physically attracted to me. Was it just a friendly lunch? Or had I said something that turned him off?

The girls and I headed to the park after dinner. They spent most of the time on the swings and I spent most of the time pushing them super high.

"Push me higher, Mommy," yelled Sofia.

"I am still higher than you, Sofia," boasted Hailey.

"Okay, girls, you're both high enough. Please hold on tight, I don't want either of you to fall. Okay?" I yelled up toward them to make sure they heard me. They were both fearless; I, on the other hand, had mom anxiety that they would fall and break something. I went back and forth pushing the girls who were having a blast on the swings while my mind went back and forth wondering if I were really the type of lady that Jonathan could be interested in romantically.

The next day before Jonathan got ready to head back home to Chicago, he came looking for me to give me his cell phone number. He looked so handsome and the butterflies in my gut felt like they were playing bumper cars the moment he approached me.

"I'm on vacation for the next two weeks, but I would love to talk to you more to get to know you better," he said, as he handed me his business card.

I raised my eyebrows in amazement that he was interested and smiled at him. I am sure my jaw dropped somewhere at that point as well, not expecting the invitation. Biting my lower lip to make sure my jaw wasn't still on the floor, I reached to take his card that he had offered me.

"I would like that," I replied as I felt my cheeks become flushed. Over the next two weeks we talked every night for hours after the girls went to bed. I told him all about myself and he listened to every word and showed interest by asking me questions throughout our conversation.

"What were your parents like when you were little?" asked Jonathan.

"Well, my parents divorced when I was in the third

grade. They fought a lot when I was little. I still remember my mom yelling constantly at my dad. My brother and I would hide in the linen closet to get away from all the screaming," I said as I recalled the memories of my parents growing up.

"Oh, so you have a brother?" asked Jonathan.

"I have a younger brother, but he is in the military and deployed, so I never see him anymore. It's been years since he has been back to Michigan. I miss him; we used to be inseparable," I said feeling melancholy that I hadn't seen my brother in so long.

"And your father, are you close with him?" asked Jonathan.

"No, not really. He was verbally abusive with everyone and sometimes physically abusive too. I remember him always trying to discipline my little miniature pincher Rambo by hitting him. I'd have to jump in front of my dog to protect him from my dad trying to strike him. I personally think he was jealous of Rambo because of the attention I gave him. I probably talk to my dad once or twice a year now. We don't have much to talk about," I replied realizing how awful that must have sounded to Jonathan that I had a poor relationship with my father.

"So, you're close with your mother then?" he replied, taking the liberty to assume my relationship with my mom.

"I live with my mother and she helps me with the girls," I answered, avoiding anything deeper, but Jonathan wasn't content with my response and continued to seek more information. The conversation was entirely based on my past that night.

"You didn't really answer my question," he said.

"I love my mom, and she has always been there for me. She is one of my best friends, but she tends to be a bit controlling at times," I replied hoping I didn't sound like I came from a dysfunctional, crazy, messed-up family.

"Controlling in what way?" Jonathan queried.

"It's nothing, I shouldn't have said controlling," I reacted, regretting I said too much too quickly.

"Kate, don't worry, we can't control our parents' behaviors. I won't think any less of you. You can always tell me anything. I won't judge, I promise."

"Well, it's really nothing, it's just that she always needs to know where I am going, what I am doing, and when I plan to get home. She always feels like she needs to discipline my girls–almost like she forgets I am their mother. I am grateful for all her help, but there have been many times I have had to bite my lip to prevent an argument," I explained feeling guilty talking about my mom in such a critical and negative way, but Jonathan was very persistent and kept pushing to know more.

"You mention friends–other than your mom, do you have any?" asked Jonathan as if he was establishing my socially awkwardness.

"I have one best friend from high school. We've grown up together since kindergarten. But she became a flight attendant and travels a lot all over the world. We rarely talk or see each other now," I responded. *Wow, I really don't know that many people,* I thought to myself. Jonathan heard my silence over the phone.

"What's wrong, Kate? Why did you go quiet?" he asked.

"Oh, no reason, just was remembering my girlfriend and got distracted," I replied, lying to him about my realization that I did not have a fun active life; I was wrapped up with my kids and work and I never made time. Jonathan continued with more questions, not giving me much of a chance to ask him anything.

"And what about your ex-husband? Is he in the girls' lives at all?" Jonathan asked, continuing to pose questions, and letting me babble on and on. He was fascinated in learning more about my history, but almost in an interviewer type of way.

"Oh, my ex-husband was my high-school sweetheart. We got married after I got pregnant with Hailey. He stuck around for a year after I had Sofia and then he wanted out to pursue his career. I always wondered if he had someone else, but I couldn't prove it," I answered, realizing how much I had disclosed to him. Jonathan had my full attention as he asked me to continue. It was refreshing for a guy to be so attentive and interested in everything I had to say. I was so busy talking and answering questions, I didn't stop to realize I hadn't been bouncing the conversation back to him at all. I hadn't asked him any questions to learn about him on a deeper level. The first night we talked for hours, and at about two in the morning, I realized I had to get up for work and we said good night. Once we hung up, I got a stream of *good night, sweet dreams, you are beautiful, xoxox* texts.

After that, every night we would talk until about midnight. In the morning I would get a barrage of amazing texts.

Some would be sweet, flattery, complimentary texts, such as...

"Good morning, beautiful. I hope you have an amazing morning. Can't wait to talk to you again tonight."

Some texts were more tender.

"Kate, I remember the first time I saw you; I made a wish to know you."

"I remember when my hand accidently brushed past

yours and we touched. That touch still brings a longing feeling in me just like it did that day and moment. I lie awake in bed at night thinking about you."

And then other texts were extremely sexual that would give me a shiver of excitement when I would read them–texts, such as...

"What color panties are you wearing? I want to remove your panties with my teeth. I am going to make love to you until you can't take it anymore."

This was certainly a new realm of dating that I had never experienced before. Like a bomb of nonstop texts had exploded on my phone. He began to come on to me exceedingly strong with provocative texts that descriptively told me what he would do when he got his hands all over me. How was a girl supposed to concentrate? As the texts rolled in over the next few weeks that we dated, they became increasingly sexual: "I am going to taste every inch of your scrumptious body. I want to give you a mouthful and let you swallow something you have never tasted before." I was addicted to receiving his texts. I would look at my phone every second, waiting for the next text. He had the power with his words to make my heart skip a beat in one sentence and become sexually aroused with another. The texts continued all evening as well. It was hard to be engaged at work during the day or focus on the girls in the evening as Jonathan continued to text. I would be at the park or helping the girls with their homework and my phone would buzz almost nonstop. My texts back to him were plain Jane. I didn't have that skill of texting seductively so usually I replied with, "Oh baby," or with a purple devil emoji. One evening I was sitting with Hailey reading and my phone that was resting on the table was vibrating with reoccurring notifications of another text message.

"Why does your phone buzz like a bee all the time now, Mommy?" asked Hailey when I would get another text.

"Oh, it's work, baby, let me answer it quickly and then let's keep reading," I replied.

"Work? You never got texts like that from work before, Kate. What is going on?" asked my mother, overhearing my conversation with Hailey.

"Mom, please," I replied. "It's not the time."

My mom narrowed her eyes as if to say, "This conversation isn't over." I ignored her and continued reading with Hailey. Sofia was in the other room watching her favorite cartoon. She and I had already read her favorite book and she was enjoying her snack as I worked with her sister.

"Okay, let's get ready for bed," I said as we finished up the book. I was trying to multitask my attention between my girls and Jonathan. The texts kept coming in and they were more and more intense and erotic.

"Kate, I can't stop thinking about your exquisite long legs. I want you to wear skirts for me from now on so I can run my fingers up those sexy legs, up your thighs, and under your skirt. I want to make you scream with pleasure."

That night after the girls went to bed, my mom approached me.

"So, tell me, who's the man?" asked my mom.

"How do you know it's a man?"

"Kate please," my mom said matter-of-factly.

"Fine. I am just getting to know a guy from work. He's a manager and a really nice man."

"Well, when do I get to meet him?" asked my mom.

"Not yet," I said, rolling my eyes and letting out an

exasperated sigh.

"How do you know who this guy is? He could be a crazy person. You have little girls to protect, you know."

"Seriously, Mom, why do you have to be so paranoid?" I replied, crossing my arms and frowning. "I am going to bed. Good night, Ma," I said as I headed for my bedroom.

"Good night, Kate," replied my mom, seemingly unimpressed she didn't have a say in my decisions.

I went to bed with thoughts of Jonathan dancing in my head. He clearly was a passionate man from everything I was seeing about him and how he engaged with me. His texts painted such a vivid picture of how he wanted me. I lay in bed rereading his texts and becoming aroused all over again. I texted him before I went to bed.

"I am rereading your texts in bed. You have a way with words."

"Really, is it turning you on? Are you in bed now? I want you to touch yourself like I plan to do when I see you."

"No, I don't do that," I texted back, feeling my heart begin to race. The phone rang and it was Jonathan. He apparently was thunderstruck and had to talk to me about it.

"What do you mean you don't do that?" were the first words he said when I picked up the phone, bypassing a "hello" greeting.

"No, I am not comfortable doing that. And hello, by the way," I answered in response to his question that he used in exchange for a positive phone greeting.

"Kate, you have to masturbate."

"That's ridiculous! Why do I have to masturbate?"

"It helps you relax, and that's how you understand

your body. It's easy. Put one hand on your breast and the other on the inside of your lips and play with yourself. I want to hear you on the phone moaning and groaning as you play with yourself."

"Wait, are you serious? Now?"

"Yes, now. I want to hear you come. Close your eyes."

I did as he asked, and as I felt myself for the first time, I realized I was experiencing enjoyment in my touch. I closed my eyes and envisioned Jonathan making love to me. I began to make moaning sounds.

"Yes, baby, that's it. Feel yourself like you want me to when I am there. I want to lick every inch of your body. I'm going to bend you over, start soft and gentle, and then finish hard and rough," he said, talking dirty to me over the phone. I continued to please myself to the point of no return. Jonathan could hear me quietly moan and then go silent.

"There, baby, doesn't that feel good?" he said after he realized I had orgasmed. I was speechless and couldn't respond as I tried to regain my brain functions.

"Good night, now you sleep," he said before he hung up.

How did he do that? I had never ever done that before. Phone sex was a first for me. The next morning, I was incredibly distracted and was having difficulty focusing at work. I was beginning to make mistakes on the job like forgetting to do my regular maintenance checks or recording the daily data from the equipment. I was too busy thinking about his texts and imagining us together. Jonathan had me in a constant dreamy state with his X-rated texts, but I loved every one of them. I was hooked. It was a bit overwhelming, but hot and sexy and nothing like what I had ever experienced. I was flattered by his kind compliments in one text and horny from another. My ex wouldn't text anything like this; it was always short, uninteresting texts like, "I will be home late" or "What's for dinner?" And occasionally he would use pet names like *babe* or *hun*.

No one was able to set my heart on fire like Jonathan could. But he didn't waste any time. From the moment we started talking, his texts went straight from "Good morning, beautiful" to "I want to feel every inch of your body with my tongue," and frankly I loved every one of them; they were incredible. Jonathan made me feel sexy and desirable. He made me feel like a woman, and I hadn't felt that way in such a long time. I didn't want that feeling to end. Was his attraction for me that strong that it provoked all these overwhelming, seductive texts? I wasn't sure, but I wanted more. I wanted to feel admired and adored. Hell, what woman doesn't, right?

I didn't understand though how a senior executive manager had the time in his busy schedule to send a continuous stream of texts the way he did, but he was on vacation. I was quite sure that the love-bombing texts would fade once he was back to work. In the meantime, I was on cloud nine. This man was checking off all the boxes of my perfect guy. *How did I get so lucky?* I thought to myself.

Jonathan was traveling to our facility off and on during the first couple weeks after his two-week vacation. That gave us the opportunity to meet for lunch occasionally. After a month of talking and having lunch, we made plans to go out on our first evening date. We arranged it so that he would pick me up after the girls' bedtime. I didn't want to introduce him to them yet since we were still early in the dating phase. The girls had never seen me with a man before other than their father, and they were too young when he left to remember him. When the quitting bell went off at work signaling the end of the shift, I rushed home. I was a ball of energy all day, enthusiastic about my date with Jonathan. All in all, the lunch dates were swell, but this was the next step, the romantic step. I could not stop thinking about what I would wear and how I was going to style my hair. When I got home, the girls fed off my mixed emotions of jitters and eagerness. They were all giggly and playful. At dinner Sofia and Hailey were high energy, bouncy, and silly.

"Kate, do you really have to fool around at the table?" asked my mom as she took a deep breath and sighed, showing her disapproval.

"Come on, Mom, the girls are just having a little dinner table fun," I replied, realizing we were clearly annoying my mother at dinner as we goofed around making googly eyes at each other.

"Okay, girls, let's finish and we will have a competition after dinner of who can make the funniest face," I said trying to appease my mother who disapproved of us being playful during dinner. Once we had finished and cleaned up the plates, the girls and I ran off to their bedroom to start our funny-face competition.

"Mommy, look at me!" Sofia shouted as she stuck her tongue out and crossed her eyes.

"My turn...look at me, Mommy!" said Hailey as she sucked in her cheeks into her lips and made a fish face.

"Wow, you girls are good at this! Let me try," I said as I pulled my mouth wide open with my fingers, stuck my tongue out, and crossed my eyes. The girls rolled over on the bed laughing and I leaned over and began to tickle them. Soon it was bedtime and I had to get ready for my date.

"Okay, girls, why don't you get your jammies on and

climb into bed," I said. The girls fell asleep almost the moment their heads hit the pillow, and I went to prepare for my date with Jonathan. I was filled with a whirlwind of emotions as I ran between the bedroom and the bathroom trying to get ready. I was nervous, excited, and full of anticipation of our first kiss. He was picking me up at nine for drinks, so I needed to get a move on. I put my earbuds in and tried to relax by listening to music as I applied my makeup and styled my hair. I missed Jonathan's text that he was here, but I heard the doorbell. I snatched my heels and purse and darted down the stairs only to find my mother getting ready to answer the door. I stepped in front of the doorknob before she could reach for it.

"I got it, Mom." I opened the door, grinning from ear to ear. Jonathan was dressed in dark-washed denim jeans paired with a black sport coat and a white button-down dress shirt. I took a deep breath as I studied how one man could possibly be so incredibly attractive.

"Hello, Jonathan," I said, smiling up at him.

"Hello, sweetie," he replied, gazing at me, and before leaning in for an embrace, he caught a glance of my mother. At that point I had no way of escaping the dreaded introduction once he noticed her peering over my shoulder.

"Jonathan, this is my mother, Beth. Beth, this is Jonathan," I said, crossing my arms and turning my body away from her.

"It's a pleasure to meet you, Jonathan," my mom said, smiling up at him. "I was anticipating that we would meet soon. Took longer than expected," said my mother in such a candid manner I was embarrassed.

"The pleasure is all mine, Beth. Kate never told me how lovely and beautiful her mother is. I see where the beauty in the family comes from," Jonathan replied as he greeted her with a warm smile. "May I have the honor of taking Kate out tonight?"

"Of course! Such a gentleman, of course, have fun," said my mom. "Maybe you can have dinner here with the family one day; I know the girls would love it." She smiled warmly taking it upon herself to invite Jonathan to dinner without first discussing it with me.

"Okay, Mom, we have to get going now." I huffed as I grabbed Jonathan's hand, not giving him a chance to reply, and dragged him away. It was noticeably clear she approved of Jonathan.

We went out for cocktails together and had a pleasant evening. Our date ended with him escorting me to my door hand in hand. I could feel the chemistry building between us and I had no doubt if I didn't have a full house, the night would have ended up with us having breakfast. Jonathan and I stopped at my door. He inched toward me slowly and backed me up against it. He was pressed into me so close I felt his heartbeat through his shirt. He rested his hands above my shoulders against the door and leaned in. He kissed me softly, and then backed up and looked into my eyes hungrily with his intense blue eyes. The chemistry unleashed and he followed with another kiss that was much harder and longer. It was passion that made my toes curl. Jonathan took my breath away during that kiss and I literally wasn't sure whether I stopped breathing or not.

"You should get some rest. I will wait for you until you are safe inside."

I searched through my purse, looking for my keys. I pulled them out and fumbled with the lock, clearly not having any cognitive abilities after surrendering to his passionate kiss.

"Good night, Kate," he said as I stepped inside my house.

"Good night, Jonathan."

When I walked in, my mother was waiting up for me, wanting to hear more about Jonathan and my date.

"Kate, he seems genuinely nice. I think this one is a keeper," my mom exclaimed with enthusiasm, not waiting one moment for me to take my heels off and put my stuff down on the entryway table. She was sitting halfway up the stairs waiting for me to come home.

"Tell me more about him. I think this is the one," she said with tears in her eyes. She was so emotional she was having trouble keeping still.

"Keep your voice down, Mom; you are going to wake the girls up. Anyway, how can you possibly say he is the one–we don't even freakin' know him well enough. And why are you are tearing up?" I replied as I leaned toward her and wrinkled my nose at her. I was puzzled as to why my mom was acting so weird and sentimental.

"Because, sweetie, I just want you to meet someone that will treat you the way you deserve to be treated. I don't want you to be alone the rest of your life."

"I am not alone; I have you and the girls," I replied, giving her a hug and kiss on the cheek. "Get some sleep, Mom. I am going to bed. I love you." I walked around the step she was sitting on and made my way up the stairs to bed.

"Okay, dear, love you too."

That next week, Jonathan wanted to take me away for a weekend getaway and asked me to see if my mom could babysit. My mom agreed to watch the girls to give us a full weekend together. She wanted to make sure I had time to get to know Jonathan because she thought he was such a catch. When Jonathan arrived at my house, he came inside and greeted my mom with a big hug. "Hello, Mrs. Davis. It is so wonderful to see you again," he said with the corner of his mouth raised revealing a handsome grin. "How are you today?" he asked politely.

"Hello, Jonathan. Please just call me Beth. I am doing well, thank you for asking."

"Thank you so much for watching Sofia and Hailey so that I can steal Kate away for the weekend," Jonathan said, maintaining eye contact with her, showing that she had his full attention.

"Absolutely! You kids have fun, you deserve it. Don't worry about the girls, Kate, we will be fine," said my mom, pushing us out the door.

"Wait, Mom, let me run upstairs and give the girls a kiss before I go." I turned to Jonathan. "Hun, can you please put my overnight bag in the car? I will be right back." I handed it to him after kissing him on the cheek. I ran upstairs to the girls' room to give them each a kiss goodbye.

"Hailey, Sofia. Come give Mommy a kiss. I have to get going," I said as I walked into their room. They both almost simultaneously said, "Mommy, why do you have to go?" They had frowns on their faces and were dragging their feet to come give me a kiss goodbye. I walked over to them and kneeled so I could talk to them at eye level.

"Girls, come on, we talked about this. It's only for one day and one night. I will be back before you know it. Plus, you will have so much fun with Grandma at the park tomorrow. I promise I will be home in no time," I said, giving them both a kiss. "Okay?" I asked wanting to hear them give me their reassurance that they were going to be okay.

"Okay, Mommy," they both said with pouty voices and sad, little puppy-dog eyes.

I left the room filled with mom guilt. I think that was the first weekend I had left them, and I hated leaving knowing they were both going to miss me. I kept going and buried my emotions; I didn't want Jonathan to confuse my feelings of missing the girls with not wanting to spend the weekend with him. I walked outside and headed toward Jonathan's car. He and my mom were chitchatting by the driver's side waiting for me to be ready.

"Okay, Mom, we will be back Sunday morning. We are at a ski resort about three hours away if anything happens and you need us to come home," I said. I then bit my bottom lip trying to keep my eyes from watering.

"Don't worry, we will all be fine, dear. Now both of you get going," my mom said, giving me a wink. I got in the car and Jonathan pulled out of my driveway honking his horn a double beep to signal goodbye as we waved.

"Jonathan, I don't know how to ski. I don't think we talked about it before you booked it," I said as we drove up.

"Oh, don't worry Kate, we won't be skiing. I plan to ravish you all weekend. We will have long, steamy, hot-tub sex, and wonderful meals in between to keep your energy up," he stated with a carefree attitude. We held hands and listened to music, while I laid my head on his shoulder as he drove. About halfway up to the lodge, Jonathan's hands slowly began to wander.

"Jonathan, focus on the road," I said, giggling and stopping his hand from making his way down my top.

"Don't worry about that, Kate, I will be all eyes on the road, but my hands don't need to be," he said as he unclasped my bra.

"Jonathan, you are so bad." I giggled at his persistence. He was quick at unhooking my bra. He had such a tender touch; I really didn't want him to stop.

The drive to the cabin was quick as Jonathan felt me up and I stroked my hands up and down his pants making him hard. It was the naughtiest car ride I had ever experienced, and by the time we made it to the hotel, we were both very turned on. We barely were able to take our hands off each other during check-in. The sexual tension was intense and noticeable. Jonathan couldn't wait to rip my clothes off and frankly I couldn't wait to help him. We headed up to get our room key from the receptionist who had a smirk on her face as she was getting us checked in.

"Will you need ski rentals for the weekend?"

"No, the key card will be all. Thank you, Amy," Jonathan replied, trying to remain formal and discreet on how horny he was.

"Yes, no problem, sir. Enjoy your stay," she said smiling at me as if to say, *I predict skiing will not be in your plans this weekend.*

The long-distance relationship had made it difficult and the chemistry was electrifying. It was built up and I could tell it was going to be a magical weekend. Jonathan and I headed straight for our room. The second we walked in he shut the door and pressed me up against it. Jonathan put both his hands around my waist and pulled me in for a long, hard kiss. As I was pinned up against the door, we worked on removing each other's clothes. He pulled down my panties and I unbuckled his pants and pulled open the zipper. I was already braless from the car ride up and the dress I was wearing made it easy for him to get access. We hadn't unlocked our lips, still tasting and exploring each other, building up the passionate sex that was about to happen for the first time as a couple.

"I want you, Kate," Jonathan said as he took a quick breath in between his long, hard kisses. He pressed his lips back onto mine and simultaneously picked me up by my ass, pulling my legs up around his waist. He walked me over to the bed, placed me down on my back, and finished pulling his pants off. I took a deep breath as he climbed on top of me.

"You feel so good and so tight."

"I'm sorry," I whispered, embarrassed.

"I love it. You are all mine." He pushed himself in even harder. I screamed as it hurt and felt good at the same time.

"Are you okay?"

"Yes, it's just been a while."

Jonathan smiled and spread my legs apart as wide as they could go.

"Just relax and open up," he whispered as he continued making slow and deep love to me.

We dated for four months, going out on evening date nights once every week or two. We didn't see each other as much as we both wanted to, but we never missed our evening talks. Things between us were starting to get more serious as we made plans about the future–marriage and even the possibility of having a child together. It was just talk as we were starting a new relationship, but we were both head over heels, and when you know it's right, you go for it. Jonathan was so attractive and exciting. He knew a way to a woman's heart–fancy dinners and flowers. It felt like a dream.

His constant attention, generosity, kindness, and sweet talk clouded me from the speed our relationship was moving.

One day, Jonathan presented me with a gift at lunch.

"What is this?" I asked, sitting up from my typical slouched posture, taking the gift into my hands.

"Just open it, you'll see," he replied, taking another bite of his lunch, acting nonchalant about his gift.

I opened the wrapped box and inside was a brand-new iPhone. I looked up at him, eyes wide open and slightly caught off guard about his choice of gift.

"A cell phone? Why are you giving me a cell phone?" I asked.

"Kate, I want to help you. I just added you to my plan. It is peanuts for me to add another line but for you it's an extra expense. Now you have one less thing to worry about. Anyway, it is bound to happen when we are together, so why not get it early to help you out?" Jonathan replied as he ran his fingers through his hair.

"Jonathan, this is incredibly thoughtful of you, but I can't accept this." I reached over the table with the box, giving it back to him. I tilted my head to the side as I processed his generosity realizing I was dating the man of my dreams. He gently pushed the box back toward me.

"It's paid for and it's a gift. I want you to have the ability to be able to communicate with me anytime without stressing about money. Take it, I won't take no for an answer. It is already set up, so you don't have any excuses." He squinted his eyes like he was waiting for me to argue with him.

"I don't know what to say. How can I thank you?"

"I am sure you can figure out a way to thank me

tonight," he said, winking at me.

I blushed and giggled. I didn't know what to think. Is this for real? What did I do to deserve such an amazing man? My prayers were finally answered. At last I had found my Mr. Right!

CHAPTER THREE
DATING BLISS

THAT NIGHT JONATHAN STOPPED BY MY HOUSE AND asked me to join him for appetizers and drinks. The night was still young. It was 8:30 p.m. and Jonathan and I had the night to ourselves. The girls had already gone to sleep for the evening after we had fun at the park running around playing tag, hopscotch, and hide-and-seek. Jonathan heard from the folks at work about a new Italian restaurant that recently opened nearby. He had chosen that as the destination for us. Apparently, they were known for their Italian wine selection and their delicious cuisine. The restaurant was in downtown Detroit in one of the historic buildings. They had valet parking service, which was always a treat when dressed up wearing heels. I wasn't accustomed to wearing heels after so many years of hard-toe boots. I felt awkward and uncomfortable walking with them, especially in the cold. The valet parking attendant opened the car door for me first before heading over to the driver's side. Jonathan didn't hesitate—he was out of the car, took his valet ticket, and with his arm around my waist, we walked into the restaurant together. It was a cozy little restaurant, but the atmosphere was chic with an added elegance that tastefully complemented the historical building.

"Good evening, dining for two?" the hostess asked as we walked in, welcoming us to the restaurant.

"Yes, please, we would like a booth," requested Jonathan.

"Yes, sir, my name is Leslie and I will be happy to show you to a table. Please follow me." She grabbed two menus and escorted us to a booth.

She was a young lady, maybe in her twenties with long blond hair. She was wearing a beautiful gray dress that accentuated her curves, and black heels that made her legs look long and toned. She walked with ease as she moved, making me feel self-conscious of my walking abilities in heels. She stopped at the booth where she had thought was a good choice, but Jonathan did not approve. "Could you please seat us away from the front of the restaurant? Could we not have that booth?" he asked, pointing to a booth in the corner near the fireplace.

"Yes sir, that's available." She picked up the menus and smiled. "Follow me, please."

The hostess escorted us to the next seating choice. She held her hand to present us with the preferred booth selection Jonathan requested. I slid into the booth seat and Jonathan immediately sat right next to me, as opposed to the opposite side of the table where the hostess was expecting. She quickly adjusted his menu so that it was facing him.

"Enjoy. Your waiter will be with you shortly to take your order." She smiled and walked off leaving us alone.

“Kate, you are the most beautiful woman in the room.” Jonathan reached for my hand. As he opened his mouth to continue, the waiter appeared.

“Hello, my name is Kenny. What can I get you to drink?” Jonathan turned toward the waiter and gave him a cold frown.

“You know it shows more class when you don’t interrupt a customer talking. Please bring us two glasses of your best red wine,” Jonathan said as his nostrils flared, and he rolled his eyes.

He quickly turned his attention back to me, and in the blink of an eye, his mood went from bothered by the waiter to sweet and romantic toward me. I felt Jonathan’s rude behavior toward the waiter was out of character. It was almost like he was upset that he had interrupted us before he could finish his compliment of me. Maybe being interrupted is his pet peeve, or was he startled by the waiter as he was attempting to have a romantic moment with me? Either way, the waiter was only doing his job. I had never seen that side of Jonathan before. Was he just having an off night, or was one of his traits starting to rear its ugly head? Should I be worried? I knew I had my own skeletons in the closet, and I was no angel, but I knew what my skeletons were. I was still learning his, and rudeness to the waiter was not favorable. Maybe he was showing his protective, jealous side. All things considered, the waiter was a handsome young man. Was that enough to make Jonathan feel threatened, making him appear cold and condescending? Maybe so! I had never had a jealous man in my life before. The girls’ father was anything but jealous. Sometimes I was almost certain my ex-husband was happy when other men were physically attracted to me. It gave him an ego boost. Jonathan was more of the conservative type from what I could tell. It was very flattering, despite how rude he appeared on the surface to other men that intimidated him.

He held my hand the entire evening as we sipped wine and ate. When he needed his hand back, he refused to dissolve our hand lock. Instead, he would switch hands. It was very affectionate yet kind of impractical and slightly possessive. Of course, that may have been due to his insecurity with the waiter. I shouldn't be criticizing the desire for physical touch. There is nothing more important between two people than the electrifying feeling of a touch or a kiss. Jonathan was particularly good at making sure he did not let go of any precious moments between us, even if it meant keeping our hands locked the entire night. We didn't see each other like other couples did that weren't in a long-distance relationship, so any moment spent alone together was precious. The waiter came back with our order, and I felt Jonathan's mood instantaneously shift with his presence.

"You need to learn to be more observant, sir; my girlfriend and I have had empty wine glasses for over ten minutes now. I expect more for the money I am paying. Please just bring us the bill," snapped Jonathan. He was demanding and acted in a contemptuous manner toward the waiter, and I slouched down wanting to hide. I felt so bad for him, but I didn't know what to do to change the situation. I wasn't good with confrontation, so all I could do was give the waiter an apologetic look and put my head down to show I didn't agree with Jonathan's behavior.

I scratched my head in confusion, leaned over, and whispered, "Jonathan, are you upset with the waiter? You're being very rude to him. Is there something wrong?"

"Don't you worry about it, Kate. Everything is fine. Let's

just get out of here."

He pulled out his wallet, covered it with both his hands, and began tapping his fingers on the table while he waited for the waiter to return. I decided not to interrupt Jonathan's impatient demeanor as he looked stern and unimpressed by the service. The waiter brought over a leather waiter wallet with the bill inside. Jonathan pulled out his platinum American Express card and placed it inside the waiter's wallet, setting it at the edge of our table. The waiter came over and picked it up.

"Thank you, sir, I will be right back with your card." He scurried off to his computer console to check us out.

I was confused by Jonathan's attitude and what triggered his behavior and rapid mood swings. I didn't want to start a fight with him about it, but I was puzzled. I sat quietly at the table wanting to go so we could continue our evening. We all have our moments and it was not something I wanted to dwell on. I watched Jonathan sign the bill and place his credit card back into his wallet. We left the restaurant and Jonathan returned to his pleasant self, holding my hand as he drove us to the hotel where he was staying while he was in Michigan. The MGM Grand Hotel was one of the top luxurious hotels in Detroit. He pulled up to the valet parking and we made our way into the hotel. Jonathan had extended his right elbow where I placed my hand through so we could walk in side by side through the automatic sliding glass doors. The hotel was stunning, filled with an aura of elegance and class throughout. The grandiose 20-foot ceilings were complimented with marble flooring and beautiful wood walls throughout. Off to one side was a stylish modern guest living room complete with a fireplace and contemporary art for guests to relax while waiting for other guests or their valet parking attendant. The lobby could easily stack ten Detroit homes from my neighborhood inside and still have room.

Jonathan and I strolled over to the elevator; our destination was the fifth floor. We walked in and I was speechless. I wasn't used to being in such an upper-class expensive hotel. The room was decorated with high-quality stylish furniture, neutral colors on the walls, and curtains that hung from the ceiling to the floor. The curtains were made of Indian gold- and maroon-colored silk and remained open to allow guests to enjoy the panoramic view of the city lights at night. Everything was perfectly in its place, from plush pillows on the sofa to the lamps on the side tables. The sheets were pressed, and the plush-top white comforter gave the impression we would be sleeping on a fluffy cloud.

Jonathan had arranged with the hotel concierge to have champagne, strawberries, and roses waiting for me. He stood back and watched me as I took in the beautiful room. After admiring the room, my eyes landed on Jonathan, whose eyes were lit up and filled with passion for me. Nothing seemed to impress him about the luxuries that surrounded him, but he seemed to be impressed or at least taken with the submissive, self-conscious lady who stood before him in his room. The atmosphere of luxury was his norm and expectation as he clearly was at ease with expensive and prestigious experiences. I, on the other hand, felt small and overwhelmed by it all. Jonathan walked over to me and passionately picked me up. His hands circled me, lifting me in the air, as my legs snaked around his waist. Kissing my neck, he gently laid me on the bed. The luxurious duvet cover on top was soft and wrapped around me, snuggling me in as I expected. He kneeled on the floor in front of me and all the texts of what he would do to me suddenly flooded into my head. He ran his hands up my skirt, followed by his tongue.

"I want to taste you, baby," he said. He pinched the material of my panties on either side of my hips and gently pulled them down my legs. I clenched the soft white duvet, preparing for what was about to happen. Jonathan removed my panties, spread my legs apart, and began to make his way back up again–this time slower, as if to make sure he didn't miss one inch of me.

"Is this what you were waiting for?" he whispered. "Do you want me, Kate? I want to hear you tell me you want me," Jonathan said in a very sexual yet almost dominating tone. He was demanding and it turned me on, making me want to do whatever he wanted.

"I want you!" I replied, quivering with anticipation. He began to tease me softly with his tongue.

"You are mine. All mine. I am going to make you want me so badly you are going to cry," he said. He moved up my thigh, making me go crazy with lust for him. I was completely aroused and began to moan with pleasure.

"I want to hear you beg for it," he demanded.

"I want you. Please don't stop!" I said as I breathed deeply and closed my eyes, taking it all in.

I couldn't take it. Jonathan took me to my peak, to the point I couldn't handle it anymore. My heart began to race, my muscles began to shudder, and I lost myself. It was so intense, it felt like fireworks had released inside of my body and suddenly I was happy and at peace. Jonathan smiled and stood up in front of me with his chin held high and shoulders arched back. He smiled with pride knowing he was the cause of my pleasure. He unzipped his pants, climbed on top of my relaxed body, and thrust inside. I was left with the feeling of being desired and I adored it.

We both lay very still under the sheets for a while, not speaking, just letting our bodies recover and enjoying the silence. We cuddled for a few hours, and I think at one point dozed off. At about one in the morning, we startled awake at the same time. Jonathan smiled at me and I couldn't help but stare into his blue eyes that had caught my eye the first time I saw him.

"You're amazing. Where have you been all my life?" Jonathan whispered. I was in heaven. I didn't want the night to end.

After about an hour of cuddling, Jonathan propped himself up on one arm and smiled down at me. "Let's take you home, sweetie, although I wish you could stay. I want nothing more than to have you here all night with me. In my arms where you belong. But I have an early flight tomorrow and you have the girls that will be waking up soon." I started to get up and Jonathan flung his leg over me. "Uh-uh. Not yet." He smiled as he finished making his way on top of me with his body. We fucked hard this time. It wasn't about making soft love. It was about making a lasting impression with deep penetration to hold us both over for the week while he was away.

The next day I was at work and Jonathan had flown out to New York on a two-day business trip. For a short time during his flight I didn't receive any texts from him, and I found myself going through withdrawals. I was so used to receiving daily affectionate, sexual texts that the silence was almost unnerving and unusual. It was refreshing to meet a man who gave me the attention I deserved. Who valued me! Who saw me as an equal! I had never had this in my previous marriage. He was not afraid to express his emotions he had toward me.

Before Jonathan headed out on his trip, he had generously given me a gift card to treat the girls to the theater. Movie night for us was always on the couch because going out was never in the budget. The night we planned to go, I managed to get off work in time to make it home by five. Sofia and Hailey were super chatty at dinner; it was almost like I hadn't seen them for months and they had built up so much to talk about. Was I that absent from their daily lives between work and going out with Jonathan?

"Mommy, instead of going out to a movie, can we stay in and watch *Barbie Mermaid*?" asked Sofia.

"Hailey, is that what you want to watch too?" I asked, making sure both girls agreed, otherwise they would argue nonstop.

"Yes, it's my favorite movie," replied Hailey in her sweet, soft voice.

I waved my arms up in the air and shouted out loud, "Okay let's make a big bowl of popcorn, grab some juice boxes, and scrunch up together on the couch and watch *Barbie Mermaid*!"

"Yeah!" the girls both cheered as they began jumping up and down beside the table.

We spent the night watching the movie, but before I started it while the girls were getting their PJs on, I sent Jonathan a quick text.

"Hey sweetie, I will be off my phone for a couple hours because I am going to watch the *Barbie Mermaid* movie with the girls." I received a text response right away from him and was taken back by his response.

"Oh, good you are using the gift card I gave you?"

"No, the girls and I decided to stay home to watch a movie."

"Wait, what? Do you not appreciate my gift?"

"No, that's not it at all, of course I do. The girls just

wanted to watch *Barbie Mermaid* tonight. It's fine, we will use it another time. Thank you for thinking of us."

"That's fine. So then if you're staying home, why can't you text?"

"I just want to give the girls my complete attention. They get mad when I am on my phone."

"Oh, aren't I more important to you than *Barbie Mermaid*," he asked, criticizing my request for some quiet time with the girls.

"Jonathan, I don't think it's too much to ask. Of course, you're important, but I don't want the girls to think I am not watching the movie with them because I am texting you."

"Have fun then," replied Jonathan and I could tell he disapproved. I replied, "thank you," but received no response, which validated my assumption. I decided to leave him alone, but the entire time I was watching the movie I was bothered and distracted. I smiled and laughed when the girls laughed, but my mind was racing a mile a minute. *He can't possibly be annoyed that I was away from my phone for a couple hours and wouldn't text. That makes no sense*, I thought. *Who would be mad about that?* The girls appeared to thoroughly enjoy themselves and I didn't let on that I was distracted with my million thoughts of why the hell Jonathan would be mad. After the movie was over, I put the girls to bed. When they fell asleep, I headed over to my room to call Jonathan, but it went straight to voicemail. My lower lip began to quiver as my mind flooded with thoughts that he was breaking up with me. I frantically began texting him to see if he would pick up.

"Jonathan, I am trying to call. The girls are asleep now."

"Are you awake?"

"Are you upset?"

"I miss you."

"Your phone is going to voicemail, so I am assuming it's off."

"Hope everything is okay? You have me worried."

I texted as I swallowed hard and held back my tears of anxiety. I didn't want anything to change. I really cared about Jonathan. The only thing that concerned me was the anxiety I would get when he got upset and would go silent. I guess I had never cared about a man so deeply, and his silence would stress me out. I didn't like upsetting him as much as I often did. I was up all night pondering and overthinking about the fact that he was silent after I asked him to give me a couple hours with the girls. Was he giving me the silent treatment? Maybe he was just being considerate, and I was freaking out about nothing. *I must stop stressing about nothing. He is a good guy; he wouldn't be upset about something so stupid.* I was the queen of overthinking and overanalyzing too much. Jonathan never ended up calling or texting back, and I finally fell asleep around two in the morning hugging my pillow as I desperately tried to envision us together. The next morning, Jonathan texted me as I was getting ready for work.

"How was your movie? Did you enjoy not having any contact with me?"

"Jonathan, you know that's not true," I replied, afraid of his response back.

"You don't realize how selfish you are sometimes. You need to work on your approach. Instead of saying you will be offline for a couple hours, making me think you are trying to ignore me, you should have just said something gentler. Next time maybe try something like, hun, if it's okay, I am going to watch a movie with the girls, I will text you when I am done. Then I wouldn't have gotten upset with you," he replied as he explained how I could have done better with my approach. "Get to work, Kate, you are going to be late. Let's talk tonight when the girls go to sleep."

"Okay, sounds good, have a good morning," I texted back. I rushed to finish getting ready, wiped the tears from my eyes so my mom wouldn't notice, and headed off to work.

We continued to text throughout the day and when I got home, I decided to take the girls to the park. I didn't dare tell Jonathan I wouldn't be able to text; instead, I texted in between pushing the girls on the swings and watching them slide down the slide. After we got home from the park, the girls showered and got into bed. I lay with Sofia and fell asleep beside her, waking up to my phone buzzing. I looked and there were a million question marks on the screen. I jumped up and fumbled to text a reply.

"Sorry, sweetie, my phone died. I am just going to bed now, call you in a minute," I texted, lying to him about falling asleep with Sofia. Jonathan thought it was a bad habit to lie with Sofia at night and I needed to quit it at once. I didn't agree so instead I avoided the topic. Sofia didn't like the dark and I don't believe a child should go to sleep scared. It wasn't something I was going to argue about. Pick your battles they say, so avoiding the topic or lying seemed like the peaceful approach. I called Jonathan and we chatted for a little while and then I decided to bring up our relationship and how fast we were moving. It had been on my mind, but with the day-to-day busyness of work and home life, I never had a good time to mention it.

"Jonathan, I am so happy, and I am having so much

fun getting to know you and spending time with you. But...umm...don't you think we are moving a bit too fast?" I asked. "I don't want to rush things."

"Kate, I understand I have come on strong, but you are incredibly special to me. I have such a strong connection with you, and I haven't met anyone like you before. I just want to show you how much you are loved," he said.

Wait, did he just say the *L*-word? I wasn't ready for that at all and lost my train of thought.

"What were we saying?" I asked Jonathan, forgetting what I was talking about.

"You're so cute, Kate. We were talking about how beautiful you are and how I am the luckiest man to have you by my side. Nobody else will ever love you more than I do."

"Aw, thank you so much, sweetie. I feel the same way," I replied, feeling like I was on cloud nine. Jonathan had a way with words. It was clear that he was crazy about me and wanted to make sure I knew it, but there was no way he was in love with me after four months. Was that enough time to fall in love with someone?

"Why don't I come over and have dinner with you, the kids, and Beth next week. Your mother did invite me. Remember?" replied Jonathan.

"Okay, next week when you're back here, we can do that." I clenched my teeth, praying that the girls would take it well. I had never introduced them to a man before. *Do I call him my friend or boyfriend? I won't worry about it for now*, I thought.

"Good night, Kate. Rest well."

"Good night," I replied. I went to put the phone down and a text with fifteen hearts popped up.

I sent a text back with hearts and he sent me kissing

emoji faces in return. I smiled and returned the same emoji faces back. Jonathan said good night, but he didn't seem to mean it. The next text came in with a line of purple devil emojis. I smiled. I sent him a purple emoji back with another "good night" text. Jonathan continued for another five minutes bouncing back emojis.

"Do you always harass young women repeatedly in the middle of the night?" I asked, teasing him.

"Only the cute ones. Good night, baby!" he replied.

"Good night, Jonathan," I texted back. I rolled over to my left side and went to sleep.

The following morning, work was terribly busy, and I had to drive to a supplier to pick up a part we needed right away to keep one of the machines running. As I was headed onto the highway, I heard my phone notify me of a text. It was a picture text from Jonathan. I couldn't open it right away until I got off the highway and at a light. I picked up my phone and opened the text and saw it was a GPS screenshot of my location. The picture showed I was on the on-ramp of Interstate 75 and there was a playful caption that read, "I see you!" followed by a wink emoji.

I was unaware that Jonathan had shared my location with his phone and had complete visibility of where I was at all time. It wasn't like I had anything to hide, but I was taken aback by the level of his spying on me and lack of trust. My phone rang, and it was Jonathan. I fumbled trying to answer it as I was driving again. I was confused and trying to gather my thoughts right at that moment on whether I should react as upset that he had been tracking me. I finally managed to swipe "accept" on my phone.

"Jonathan, why are you tracking me? I don't

understand, do you not trust me?" I asked in a brittle voice, alarmed at the fact that he was secretly tracking me and that he even felt the need to do so. I could sense his mood change through the phone right away when I questioned him.

"Wow, Kate, I was just joking. Don't be so overdramatic. I was only trying to brighten your day with a joke, but clearly you can't take one. Anyway, how could you say that I don't trust you? That's just hurtful," he said, defending himself.

Just like that, I found myself feeling guilty and apologizing to him. I hadn't realized how accusatory I had sounded. Why was I starting a fight with him? I should have never alluded that he didn't trust me–that wasn't like me; I had never done that before. I could only guess I was not used to being in a relationship with so much communication or having a man in my life again. I needed to stop being so paranoid. I got that from my mother. Why would he be tracking me, anyway? He had no reason to suspect me of anything.

"I'm so sorry, Jonathan, I shouldn't have accused you of spying on me. Of course, you were joking. I don't know what I was thinking," I said. I felt terrible for even thinking ill of Jonathan after all he had done for me.

"It's fine, Kate. Is everything okay?" he asked.

"Yes, I'm good. I am on my way to a supplier. One of our machines needs a part right away before it breaks down. Can I call you tonight?" I asked softly in a crackling voice wanting to run away from feeling so stupid and guilty for being so judgmental.

"Yes, drive safe," Jonathan responded and then I heard the phone click.

How can I overreact like that? Stop it, Kate, you are going to ruin a good thing, I lectured myself.

The following week Jonathan was back in Detroit for a couple days. We made plans for him to come over for dinner so he could finally meet Sofia and Hailey. I had to still meet Scott, but he spent so much time at his mother's house there weren't many opportunities according to Jonathan. Jonathan came over at 5 p.m. for dinner. He rung the doorbell, and when I went to answer, the girls came running up behind me with my mother trailing, excited to greet him.

"Hello, sweetie," I said when I opened the door. Jonathan stood there with a freshly cut bunch of flowers and two gifts wrapped in pink wrapping paper. My mom peeked her head over my shoulder. "Come on in, Jonathan." She invited him, not giving me a chance to do so myself.

The girls were grinning from ear to ear, with their eyes popping out of their heads with the sight of presents. Jonathan looked down at them smiling.

"Well, hello there. What are your names?" he asked with the one corner of his lip slightly raised to reveal a grin.

"I'm Sofia."

"I'm Hailey and I am the oldest."

"Well, what a coincidence, I happen to have found these two gifts in my car for little girls. I think these are meant for you," Jonathan said.

"Yippee!" they both squealed with delight, as they jumped up and down in front of Jonathan. Jonathan handed each one a gift, and as they ran off, they started giggling and laughing.

"Just stop right now, girls. What do you say to Jonathan?" I sternly asked them, stopping them both dead in their tracks.

"Thank you, Jonathan," the girls both said almost

in sync. They both swiftly turned around and took off running again to the living room. We all followed them to watch them reveal what they got. I smiled and leaned over to Jonathan. "You are going to be their best friend now," I said, giggling.

The girls ripped open their gifts and each pulled out their very own Barbie and Barbie Convertible Toy Vehicle, one pink and one purple. The girls were overjoyed and neither of them could contain themselves, letting out playful girlish screams. They were both in heaven.

"Wow, Jonathan, you shouldn't have. You spent a lot of money," I said as my cheeks turned pink.

"It's fine, Kate, I never had little girls of my own; buying for them was fun," he said. I didn't want to be weird about it, but I was suddenly feeling jealous. I stood there wishing I could afford to buy gifts like that for the girls to see their over-joyous reaction from my presents. But I was being silly. Jonathan was sincere and thoughtful, and I couldn't let my mom guilt ruin that.

"Girls, what do you say to Jonathan?" I asked.

"Thank you!" they both said, running up to him and giving him a big hug.

"We love it!" said Sofia.

"Are you staying for dinner?" asked Hailey.

"You're welcome, girls. Yes, I am staying for dinner if that's okay?" Jonathan said, giving them both a hug back.

"Yeah!" they screamed with their hands up in the air.

"Go have fun," he said to them as we all headed into the kitchen to talk and get dinner ready while we let the girls play with their new toys.

"So, Jonathan, tell me about your family," asked my

mom as she tried to get more details about Jonathan.

"My mom and dad are from Chicago. My mom is a teacher and my dad's an electrical engineer. I don't have any siblings. I have been divorced a couple years now and have a fifteen-year-old son," Jonathan replied.

"And where do you see yourself in the next five years?" probed my mother.

Before Jonathan could answer, I interrupted.

"Mom, let's stop with the fifty-question interrogation and get dinner on the table. Jonathan, can you grab the potatoes for me?" I said, breaking up my mom's CIA covert investigation over Jonathan.

We all sat down for dinner, and the girls chatted nonstop about their gifts.

"Girls, you're doing more chatting than eating." My mother scowled.

"It's fine, Mom, they are just excited. Let them be," I replied, looking back at the girls with a reassuring smile.

Jonathan didn't say a word. He ate quietly at the table, keeping his head down toward his food.

"Jonathan, dear, would you like another drink?" asked my mom, breaking the bit of tension between us over the girls.

"Yes, please, Beth," replied Jonathan.

"Mommy, can Sofia and I be done now?" asked Hailey. "We want to go play."

"Yes, of course, sweetie. Take your plates into the kitchen for me, okay?" I replied.

My mother came back with Jonathan's refill and we chatted for a little longer.

"Jonathan, what is Chicago like? I have never been there. Do you own a home there?" asked my mother.

"You will have to come for a visit so I can show you around, Beth. There's lots to do. I live off a golf course. The girls would love it. I have a huge pool with a slide in the backyard," Jonathan said, taking advantage to brag a modest amount to my mom for bonus points.

"Wow, sounds lovely, Jonathan. I look forward to it," replied my mom with both eyebrows raised.

"I am delighted you and Kate met. You both are so good together. I can see the love she has for you when she looks at you. Let me leave you two lovebirds alone. I am going to retire in front of the TV," announced my mother as she stood up. "Jonathan, I am so happy you were able to join us for dinner tonight. I hope we will get to see you more often."

Jonathan stood up and leaned in to give my mother a hug. "It was my pleasure, Beth. You can count on it."

We chatted for a little longer and then Jonathan decided to call it a night. "I am going to head out and leave you to put the girls to bed. I must fly out early in the morning. Will you walk me to my car, sweetie?"

"Sure, let me just let my mother know." I walked back toward the living room and peered in.

"Mom, I am going to walk Jonathan out. Be right back to get the girls ready for bed," I said. My mom nodded while keeping her eyes glued to the television show she was watching.

When I returned to Jonathan, he took me by the hand, and we walked out to his car. When we got to the driver's side Jonathan spun me around so I was facing him. Then, cupping the back of my neck with his right hand and my butt cheek with his left hand, he pulled me close and kissed me hard. He held me tight, giving me a mind-blowing kiss that made me weak in the knees, and then let me go.

“Be good,” he said, as he got in his CTS and drove away.

CHAPTER FOUR
ISLAND BOUND

THEY SAY TIME FLIES WHEN YOU'RE HAVING FUN. Jonathan and I had now been dating for six months and it felt like we just met yesterday. On our anniversary, which also happened to land on my birthday, Jonathan told me he had a surprise for me and asked me to wear a nice dress. I wore a very tight-fitting, V-neck black mini dress with a flirtatious flare at the bottom that moved with me as I walked to show off my legs. I styled my long hair with wavy beach curls and placed a red hairband to complement my red high heels. I wanted to be a bit of a tease tonight by adding some anticipation with my sexy, slightly revealing dress. Keep his interest piqued so that his only thought all night was how much he wanted to make love to me. Jonathan picked me up at 7:30 p.m. for our date. On our drive there he had a big smile on his face from ear to ear. He leaned over and said, "You look beautiful, my love," as he placed his hand on top of my knee. I looked up at him, blushed, and rested my hand on top of his. His touch always made me get a fluttery sensation in my stomach and I loved it.

"Thank you," I said, smiling humbly. Normally I

struggled to accept compliments, but I was hoping he would take notice of my outfit.

When we arrived at the restaurant, Jonathan asked for a corner booth and ordered us two glasses of their best wine. He requested once the wine was brought to our table that we weren't bothered until we waved over a waiter.

What did he have up his sleeve? I thought. He mentioned earlier before picking me up he had a surprise for me. Was it for my birthday?

"So, what's the surprise–tell me–I can't wait. You know how impatient I am," I said, bursting eagerly with anticipation.

Amused with my excitement and enthusiasm Jonathan smirked.

"Kate, it's been six months and I wanted to tell you how much I have enjoyed our time together, and how important you have become to me. I want to give you your birthday present tonight. I hope you like it."

Jonathan handed me an envelope. "Open it," he said with confidence.

I looked up at him and then down to the sealed envelope I was holding in my hand. I ripped open the envelope and pulled out two tickets for a four-day trip to Barbados. Just for the two of us.

"Oh, my goodness, Jonathan, is this for real? A trip to Barbados? Thank you so much! This is the most amazing, extravagant gift anyone has ever given me." I shrieked with delight. I jumped out of my chair and flew around the table to give him a huge hug. "Pinch me, I want to make sure I am not dreaming," I said to him.

Jonathan smiled. "You're not dreaming, baby. Come sit down beside me. I am going to do better than pinch you; I am going to make sure you can't walk straight for a week," he said. I sat down beside him, still giggly and gleaming with excitement. I then realized–four days–that was a long time away from the girls. They had a hard time the one weekend that I was only gone for two days. Jonathan noticed my facial expression change as I stared off into space thinking.

"Are you okay, Kate? You look worried? Are you disappointed?" he asked.

"I am...wait....no, I'm not. I just realized I need to figure out what I have to do for Sofia and Hailey while I am gone for four days," I replied, looking down at the tickets in my hands.

"We will figure all that out this week. For now, don't stress about it," he said as he leaned over to give me a kiss. Under the table where no one could see he had also begun sliding his hand up my skirt. I pulled away; I didn't expect him to make a move right there in public.

"Jonathan, not here. We are at a restaurant," I said under my breath as I placed my hand on top of his to stop him from going up farther. I smiled up at the room so no one would notice his intentions, but my heart was racing a mile a minute at the thought that someone would see what he was doing.

"Kate, put your hand down. Live in the moment and enjoy. It's your birthday. I am going to give you a small preview of what is in store for you tonight," he softly demanded under his breath as he pushed his hand past mine, continuing his way up under my panties. He whispered into my ear, "Remove these."

I was very hesitant and uncomfortable about fulfilling his request. It wasn't in my nature to be so adventurous. I didn't at first do anything while shaking my head back and forth in disagreement.

Jonathan wasn't taking no for an answer. "Remove

them. I want my thank you now," he ordered. I did as he suggested very discretely. I was a shy good girl in nature, but the naughty girl came out when I was with him and it was exhilarating. I felt very aroused about doing something forbidden in public. Jonathan smiled, holding his wine glass in one hand while his other hand was under the table. He gently lifted my leg and placed it on top of his thigh. He now had me wide open and exposed using the tablecloth to cover up his intentions to tease me and feel me up. He slowly began to touch me softly, his fingers exploring ever-so gently. I remained completely still, almost frozen, not knowing what I should do. I bit my bottom lip to keep from making any moaning noises out loud. This was a classy restaurant, but it didn't make a difference if it wasn't–this was still completely testing my boundaries.

"You feel so soft, Kate." His voice was as gentle as his touch. "I knew you were a bad girl just waiting to be released." He continued fingering me, determined to feel me orgasm. I swallowed hard, trying desperately to enjoy the sensation, but focused all my energy trying not to scream with delight. I couldn't believe this was happening. He was pleasuring me under the table and all I could think about was how I wanted to rip my clothes off and have him fuck me right there. I quietly moaned in a quivering voice.

I let him continue as I tried desperately to keep my composure, keeping my face down so that no one could see my facial expressions; meanwhile my heart was pounding so hard it felt like it was going to jump out of my chest. I began to feel my body quiver as I tried to keep from letting out all kinds of sexual noises. All I wanted to do was lie down and scream for more. This was torture.

Why here? Why now? I thought.

My body wanted more, but my mind was fighting the thought of how inappropriate this was.

"Please stop, Jonathan," I begged softly.

Jonathan began to hum quietly while he continued to play with me under the table. He was enjoying watching me squirm while begging him to stop. He didn't stop, he wouldn't stop. His goal was to see me release whether I wanted to or not. I couldn't handle it any longer; the sensations were too strong. I gave in, my body and muscles tensing. I closed my eyes as I fought to internalize my orgasm. Jonathan smiled. He had done what he had set out to do, slid my leg back, licked his fingers clean, and casually waved his hand for a waiter to come over to take our order.

"Straighten up, Kate. You need to eat to regain your energy for tonight. I am not done with you," he said. We ate dinner; I was content and quietly ate. Jonathan drove us back to his hotel after dinner and made sure I showed him how grateful I was for his gift multiple times that evening.

The trip to Barbados was the following weekend and I spent the whole week preparing my mom to watch the girls while I made sure I had clothes to take to the beach. We were flying out Friday and flying home Monday, so I was only missing two days of work, and my mom was all set to be with Sofia and Hailey, so it was perfect planning on Jonathan's part. Friday came quickly and we were on a plane to Barbados.

Jonathan had purchased first-class tickets. This was an extravagance that I had only seen in the movies, but I myself never expected to have the opportunity to enjoy. These were the luxuries in life that I had only dreamed of, never expected to indulge on anytime in my lifetime.

The trip was quick from Michigan, and the hotel was extremely organized and efficient in getting us checked in when we got there so we could enjoy our day in the sun. The first day of our vacation should have been an indication that I needed to look at our relationship closer. I had only been with one man and we dated right out of school, so I never really knew what red flags to look for that indicated toxicity in a relationship. Jonathan had a quality about him that had dual personalities at times, and I was still learning them.

We were headed to the beach that day. I had brought two different sunscreens with me, SPF5 and SPF50. Jonathan said he burned in the sun quickly due to his fair skin, and I desperately wanted a tan. My legs were so pale from Michigan winters that I was sure they could glow in the dark. We walked over to the cabana bar first to grab some drinks to take with us to the beach. Jonathan asked for a local Barbados beer and I wanted a piña colada. Jonathan leaned into the bartender, spoke a few words with him and gave him a fist bump before we left with our drinks.

“What did you say to him?” I asked.

“I told him to keep them coming and I would make it worth his while,” he replied with a smirk on face. Sometimes he could be a bit lofty, but I guess that came with success.

With our drinks in hand, we walked down to where the resort had several lounge chairs and put our stuff down on a couple free ones resting next to a palm tree. We placed towels on the chairs, and I pulled out the sunscreen.

“Ahh, now this is heaven,” I said feeling lighthearted. “I love the feeling of soft white sand in between my toes, the waves crashing in front, and the sun beaming down warming me up. *It can’t get better than this.* “Would you like me to apply some sunscreen on your back, sweetie?" I asked Jonathan as I pulled out the sunscreen from my beach bag.

"Yes, please, and later you can rub your hands elsewhere when we get back to the room," he teased.

"You are very good with your hands," he said as I rubbed SPF50 on his back. "I plan to make sure to lube you up when we get back to the room and get you nice and wet," he continued with his flirtatious, dirty talk.

I blushed. "Is sex always on your mind?" I asked him.

"Of course, with a hot lady like you beside me in that bathing suit, it's hard not to think of anything else," he replied.

"You're so funny." I finished applying sunscreen on his back and then I began to apply my SPF5 Hawaiian coconut tanning lotion on myself.

"Hey hun, can you please apply some on my back?" I asked as I gave him my sunscreen.

Jonathan looked at the bottle I handed him, and his mood shifted right away from flirty to cold.

"What are you doing, Kate? Why are you only applying SPF5?" he questioned with a concerned voice. "You are going to burn. This isn't Michigan sun you know."

"I will be fine, Jonathan; I want a tan. I will make sure I put lots on," I replied.

"Didn't you tell me you burned like a lobster when you were younger during a family vacation?" Jonathan replied, recalling a conversation we had during one of our evening talks. I was happy he was listening to me and interested, but why was he using it against me to start a fight?

"Jonathan, it's not like I am twelve years old. I think I can take care of myself, *Dad*," I said jokingly, followed by a fake, sarcastic laugh. I put my sunglasses on and lay down, ignoring his silly attempt to be protective over me. *What was his problem*, I thought. I didn't understand why he felt he needed to control such a small thing. Jonathan got extremely frustrated when I didn't take his advice.

"Fine, if you are just going to ignore me and ruin our vacation, I am not going to stay." He jumped up and stormed off, leaving me at the beach by myself.

What the heck? Is he seriously mad about sunscreen?

I was struggling to understand his temper tantrum. I gathered up my beach stuff and began to chase after him, calling his name so he would stop. One of the hotel workers who had witnessed Jonathan storm off interrupted my chase.

"Is everything all right, madam?" he asked with a concerned smile.

"Yes, thank you," I replied as I continued to run after Jonathan to find out what that was all about.

It wasn't easy to run in sand with flip-flops, so I let him storm off and I slowed down to reflect on what was happening. *Is he having second thoughts about us? It seems like such a little thing, but this must be a sign he isn't happy because no one flips out about sunscreen*, I thought as I went over the fight in my head.

I got up to the room and was instantly on the defense, which turned into me yelling.

"What the heck was that all about? I can't believe you just left me there and walked away from me! You are not my father. I have one of those and we don't get along!" I yelled when I walked in. "You started a fight for no reason on the beach–why? Because you're a control freak? And then you left me stranded–who does that to their girlfriend?!"

Jonathan looked up from his phone, walked out onto the patio, and sat down, while continuing to flip through his phone and giving me the cold shoulder. I got so frustrated he wasn't engaging in the argument, I left and went to the bed. I flopped down and began to cry. Jonathan heard me crying in the other room and came in; he sat down beside me and began rubbing my back.

"Hun, I just don't want you to get burned and ruin your first vacation you have had in years. The Barbados sun is very strong, and you don't have a base tan. You have to take care of yourself or you will burn, love. You weren't listening to me. It was your fault I left. I couldn't stay there and watch you hurt yourself," he explained as I was sobbing.

Somehow, I felt guilty that I got upset for overreacting with him. He wasn't being a jerk; he was being protective of me and I took it the wrong way. I was not used to someone who offered their opinion. Of course, I overreacted. He was just being his sweet self and looking out for me. *What is wrong with me? Why am I trying to mess things up?* But still, I didn't think he should have stormed off like that, leaving me on the beach. It was embarrassing. That worker must have thought we were a crazy couple.

That night as I lay in bed after we had made love, I thought about that day and our first big fight. It was good that we had a fight, all couples have fights, it just means we are passionate but must find a way to approach each other better. We would learn that the more time we spent together. I knew I had gotten super mad and I had apologized for that, but the more I thought about it, the more I realized Jonathan hadn't admitted he was wrong. I was the one who was always taking responsibility for our fights. But he shouldn't apologize for being protective of me either. Did he love me that much and was just that protective over his girl, or did Jonathan have a controlling side that he was holding back? Despite everything, our relationship was going so fast–did I even know as much as I thought I did about him? All he had shown me was his sweet, loving side. It really had only been six months. It had been a whirlwind relationship, but he was a good guy and new relationships took time to learn about each other, so I just needed to be patient.

The next morning, we walked back down to the breakfast restaurant by the beach. It was very relaxing, drinking coffee in front of the ocean. When we came back to the room, I began to change into my bathing suit. Jonathan, who was already relaxing on the bed, said, "What do you think you are doing, young lady? Take that off and come to me; I want to have my way with you." He had already been undressing me with his eyes, and he had the look of a wild cougar about to pounce on his prey. I was instantly turned on; I went to him. The "young lady" nickname he suddenly used was something new, but I was sure it was not meant to be demeaning and more of a role-playing name for me as he played the man screwing the younger, attractive lady he just met. He was extremely passionate and intense that day, and I fell asleep after complete ecstasy and exhaustion. The one nice thing about this vacation was I didn't have my girls, so sex and naps was pretty much the main theme of the trip.

Our vacation was only four days, and on the third day of our vacation, I told Jonathan I was going to call the kids to see how they were doing. It was the first time they had been without me for such a long time and I wanted to check on them.

"I bought this trip to be alone with you, Kate, and all you can do is think about your kids," he said.

"That's not true, Jonathan. I just thought I would say hello quickly for five minutes," I replied.

He was so angry about a five-minute phone call; I just wanted to say hello and tell them I missed them. I found myself apologizing, although this time I was apologizing to make peace. It was a new relationship and this trip was about spending time together, not fighting about stupid things. Instead of fighting, I decided to sneak into the bathroom when we were on the beach and call the girls to see how they were doing. I really shouldn't have had to be sneaking around for something so small, but it wasn't worth upsetting Jonathan. This was such an extravagant gift he gave me for my birthday, I wanted to make sure he knew how appreciative I was. I didn't want to ruin our trip, but I couldn't go long without talking to Hailey and Sofia. *Choose your battles*, they say. It wasn't worth the fight, and what he didn't know wouldn't hurt him, right?

The last of the vacation was very repetitive. We had sex in the morning, afternoon, and evening. He was highly active in bed and he always made sure I was taken care of before he climbed on top to finish. It was like a honeymoon, except the expectation to have sex three times a day became a cyclical pattern. He certainly had high energy and a high libido, which was incredible and unusual for most men, but it didn't seem like it was at all about pleasing me; it really felt like he needed to have sex to fulfill his supply of acceptance and attention. What I meant is that it was like he needed to prove he was good, like he was trying to fulfill his manhood. Maybe I was reading into it too much, but I had never been with a man that would take it personally if he couldn't make me orgasm. I can't speak out of experience because I had only been with one man in my life, but my gut feeling of it being more about him trying to prove his greatness and less about the intimacy we were expressing was strong. There were many times during sex when Jonathan would ask me to repeat how wonderful he was. Was this just a guy thing? Maybe? Ultimately, I guess guys want to feel like they are pleasing their woman.

"Kate, tell me, tell me I'm the best you have ever had." I would tell him what he wanted to hear, and he would get off on knowing he was my greatest experience. It became an expected script and his sexual preference that I tell him he was the best before he orgasmed. Like it put him over the edge. *Is he proving his manhood to me or to himself?* Frankly, I couldn't tell. *Do I approach this topic with him? No, that would be greatly offensive toward his manhood and make him self-conscious during sex. Should I question his sexual expectations, or just enjoy the ride, because no one can keep this pace up for long? It's completely natural for a man to want to impress his lady, right?* And it sure felt wonderful to have that many orgasms. My body had never experienced such a roller coaster of emotions, and soon we would go back to Detroit and we wouldn't get this couple time so why not enjoy it? I felt like I was dating a horny teenager that wanted to make out with his girlfriend every minute we were together. I must admit, it was exciting and exhausting all at the same time.

CHAPTER FIVE
On Bended Knee

OUR VACATION CAME TO AN END AND WE FLEW back to Detroit. The trip was bittersweet; I loved the warm, tropical weather and being on the beach, but I was ready to be home again. I missed my girls terribly; I had not been away from them since that weekend trip so I was having Hailey and Sofia withdrawals. Jonathan landed in Detroit and then took another plane back to Chicago. He had to be back for a series of important meetings and presentations. I didn't see him physically, but Jonathan made sure to text me almost every minute of the day. From the moment I woke up there was a good-morning text–anything from how his meeting was to what he was thinking. He was an excellent communicator through text when he wasn't with me. Texts would roll in all day long.

"How is your day going, Kate? I just had one meeting after the next. I hope you feel more relaxed now that you had some time on the beach."

"I wish I was there; I miss you lots. I have a hard time sleeping now when I am away from you."

I unfortunately was extremely busy at work after taking a week off, so it was getting difficult to keep up with his texting momentum.

How was he managing to bombard me with so many texts and still get his work done? He asked me questions about my day, and he loved asking me what color panties I was wearing. I did notice when I wasn't able to text back, he would send me a million question marks, almost to say *why you aren't replying, where did you go?* I wasn't really used to being in constant communication with a person like this and it became a bit overwhelming, so I mentioned it to Jonathan that night. He would understand; it was not like I sat in an office environment. The factory floor was dangerous. Forklift trucks were moving everywhere so you couldn't be looking at your phone texting.

"Jonathan, I am sorry, but work is absolutely crazy right now. I can't always text back right away. I am on the floor most of the day," I explained. Jonathan didn't reply; he stayed quiet and I could tell he was upset. I could almost feel his shift in mood over the phone. There was a silent pause for a moment.

"That's fine, Kate, I was just trying to stay in touch while I am away, but if it's a bother to you, I will stop." His voice cut through me.

"No, it's not a bother, that's not what I meant. I love our texts; I just want you to know I can't always text back right away," I said, desperate for him to understand.

I was just trying to be honest with my concerns, but it was clear Jonathan got defensive when I did. I needed to figure out the best way to approach him, so he didn't feel challenged when I wanted to discuss a topic of concern. I changed the subject to see if we could continue our nightly enjoyable conversations but my bringing up my concern with his texts seemed to kill the mood for any new topics for the rest of the night. I didn't know how to lighten the mood, so I decided to end the conversation the best way I knew how.

“I am exhausted tonight. I think I am going to get some sleep.”

“Good night, sleep well,” he said, sarcasm seeping through his words as if he knew I was just letting him go because of our disagreement. He hung up before I could reply.

I was confused by Jonathan’s attitude to us having a conversation about a topic I wanted to address, but maybe I had picked a bad time to do that. We both had long days at work, and his stress level was high with the pressures of his job. I should probably have been more aware of my timing. My attempt to have a serious conversation about my concerns just resulted with my boyfriend becoming offended by the way I approached him. That’s it–it’s all about approach I guess, but I was certain that Jonathan did not take criticism or me approaching him with problems very well.

We continued courting and Jonathan traveled nonstop to Michigan Monday to Friday, but his assignment was nearing its completion date and corporate told him that in six weeks he was no longer required to travel to Michigan. Jonathan told me about the company’s decision, and when he noticed the panic in my face, he took me by my hand and said, “Don’t worry, Kate, I will never let you go. We will be together. I will save you and take you away. You mean too much to me to change that.” It was my romantic fairy tale coming true. My knight in shining armor coming to rescue me. He loved me, valued me, and wanted a future with me. What else could I ask for?

The following week, Jonathan came back to Detroit. He had made plans and told me to pack an overnight bag and to bring an evening dress because we were going to a show. My mom was immensely helpful, and she watched the girls so I could have some time with Jonathan. She was fond of him and realized that our relationship was serious and was headed toward a lifelong commitment. Jonathan picked me up and drove us back to the MGM Grand Hotel. It was where he stayed during the week, so I didn't suspect anything different. We arrived at the hotel early and went up to the room he booked for the weekend to get ready for the show.

Jonathan told me it was a surprise, but that we had to be ready by seven that evening. When I walked into the hotel room, I was taken back by the magnificent bouquet of three-dozen long-stemmed red roses filled with leatherleaf ferns and baby's breath sitting in the middle of the coffee table. When I turned to hug him, I was surprised to see him down on one knee ready to propose.

"Kate, the first time I got married it was because my girlfriend was pregnant, and I had to make her an honest woman. Now I know what love truly is and I want to marry you. I can't imagine my life without you." He slipped a two-carat solitaire diamond ring on my finger.

Before the ring slipped all the way down my finger, I squealed, "Yes!"

It was the most beautiful rock I had ever seen in my life. It was a solitaire diamond ring surrounded by a halo of small accent diamonds. I jumped up, wrapped my arms around Jonathan's neck, and kissed him. His lips pressed into mine, telling me with each kiss how much he desired me, which led to us making love. We had some time after getting ready, but we needed to get moving because Jonathan had purchased Broadway tickets to *The Phantom of the Opera* for that evening to celebrate our engagement. It was a magical night with the hotel, the flowers, the engagement, and the show, but in the back of my mind I felt like there was something missing. Was it me? Was it that I needed more time? I cared for Jonathan, but did I care for him enough to spend the rest of my life with him? I was attracted to him and he obviously could provide for me and the girls, but something was off with our relationship. What could possibly be missing? Jonathan was an amazing man who adored me, and had just proven so by giving me the biggest diamond ring that had only ever existed in my dreams. The entire evening was amazing, but after we returned to the hotel, we ended up in an argument. I had picked up my phone to call my mom to tell her the happy news and Jonathan got extremely annoyed.

"Are you kidding me right now?" he snapped.

"What? I am just calling my mom to tell her about the engagement, what's the problem?"

"You can tell her when we get back. No cell phones during our couple time. This time is precious, and we don't get enough of it," he replied.

He took the phone from my hand, threw it down on the coffee table, and walked away to the bathroom. I stood there speechless with my mouth wide open. I couldn't believe what he just did. I got all emotional and started to cry. I felt like a five-year-old that he had reprimanded. My mom was the one person who had been there for me during everything I went through in my life and I just wanted to tell her. Jonathan came back into the room and realized that I had broken down into tears and was emotional. This was supposed to be such a magical day and here I am crying. Jonathan came over and sat down beside me.

"Don't cry, everything will be all right. Let's get some rest. Tomorrow you can tell your mom our big news," he said. "You know what will make you feel better?"

He didn't give me time to answer as he slowly kneeled in front of me, spread open my legs, and began to kiss me. He knew exactly where to put his tongue and finger to make me forget the world. Jonathan slowly worked his magic on me and once again my heart began to beat faster; I started breathing heavily and was able to forget all my worries.

"Oh, Jonathan, that's it. Right there, don't stop!" I screamed as I hit my peak. Jonathan knew he had done his job. He stood up, climbed on top, and took his turn. Tonight really needed to end with lovemaking. We had just had a romantic evening with flowers, dinner, and a show. I sometimes messed things up by not thinking about our relationship. I was being ridiculous to want to interrupt our evening by calling my mom. I needed to start thinking more about us as a couple. Jonathan was right; there was no reason I couldn't wait until the next day. I was sure my emotions took over and he was a very patient man, which was why I was such a lucky lady to have him in my life.

Jonathan and I were now officially engaged. I never in my wildest dreams thought I would be dating again, never mind engaged to a handsome, successful, smart man that loved me as much as he did. My life was slowly turning around, and it was my turn to find true love with someone who respected me, valued me, and loved me like I had always wanted.

We woke up to get ready to leave and he stopped me and said, "Why are you getting dressed? Let's fool around one more time before we go. Once we are back, we won't be alone. Your mom and the girls will be with us the whole time."

I couldn't deny my fiancé his needs or my own, so I looked at him, smiled, and went back to bed with him.

This time, Jonathan decided to try something different. He pulled out a blindfold. He smiled at me and placed it over my eyes.

"Kate, you have been bad," he whispered as he placed his hands on my shoulders and thrust me back onto the bed.

"Oh, Jonathan, you want to play rough," I said in a sexy voice. Jonathan crawled on top of me, unzipped his pants, and gave me a mouthful.

"No talking, Kate," he said.

He placed his hands on my breasts and squeezed and slapped them. I had my mouth full and couldn't talk, but I understood that was the rule for this morning's play. Jonathan pleasured himself inside my mouth, and at that moment, with one swift move, he turned me onto my stomach and slapped my butt cheek. He slipped in to feel me inside and then pulled out and used his fingers again as he slapped my butt multiple times. He had magic fingers and, unexpectedly, he bit me.

"Do you like it rough, young lady?" he asked me as he slapped my butt cheeks again. I moaned and groaned so that he knew very well I was enjoying his new moves.

The small amount of rough play, along with not being able to see anything or speak, completely turned me on. I screamed and climaxed so quickly I learned that morning I liked the new play. Jonathan wasn't done with me once he knew I had orgasmed. Once he finished me, he spread my legs wider and took another turn while I was still on my stomach. *Wow! Where is all this coming from and what an exhilarating way to end this weekend!*

We drove back to my house to show my mom my engagement ring and tell the kids the news. It was supposed to be the happiest moment of my life, and yet we had a fight about me communicating with my family. The sex was outstanding, and he loved to make it interesting in bed, but I was not sure why I was worried about marrying him. I was just nervous. It was a big decision and of course I would have cold feet, but he treated us well and it would be the beginning of a new life for all of us.

Shake it off, Kate, I thought. *We will be great together; I just know it!*

CHAPTER SIX

SILENCE SPEAKS VOLUMES

JONATHAN WAS NOW MY fiANCé AND MY NEW BEST friend, and I wanted to tell him everything. It was a whole new level of communication that I didn't have with my ex-husband. I hadn't dated many men in my lifetime–as a matter of fact, he was the second man I had ever been in a relationship with or even intimate with–so I didn't have a lot of experience with how men acted, but Jonathan seemed to have specific expectations in his partner. He seemed to presume I would say and do things in a certain way that I hadn't learned yet and if I didn't do them, he would become somewhat irritated and show childish behaviors.

The first time I really saw this was the one evening when we were having our usual chat. We had been texting back and forth all day and I told him I was going out with my friends for lunch.

"Hey sweetie, having lunch with friends today. Can't wait to talk to you tonight. Call you after Sofia and Hailey are asleep," was all that I mentioned until that evening when he asked me about lunch.

"So how was your lunch with your friends today?" he asked.

"It was fun, I went out with the guys to celebrate one of them retiring. Known him forever."

"Wait....what? Why didn't you tell me who you were going out with? Were there any girls there or just guys?" he snapped as if I had done something horrible.

"Oh, come on, Jonathan. You know I only work with men," I replied, disregarding his silly comment of girls being there. "It's no big deal, we usually go out once a month for lunch, but it's been so busy at the steel mill that we haven't in a while," I said, but Jonathan blew his top and that was one of many silent treatment tantrums I had experienced.

"I can't believe you're keeping things from me. I should have known this. Here I am thinking you're with a couple girl coworkers and you're out having lunch with a bunch of men. I can't talk to you right now." Jonathan hung up the phone before I had a chance to reply. After that, he ignored all my calls and texts. I barraged him with frantic text messages. I couldn't understand what the big deal was that I went out for lunch.

"What did I do wrong, hun?"

"Why are you upset with me? It was just lunch with my coworkers."

"I wasn't hiding anything; I was going to tell you when we talked."

"Jonathan, please pick up the phone. Or at least text me back."

"We need to talk. I can't stand when you ignore me."

"Please reply."

"I don't handle silence well. It drives me crazy."

"I love you."

I continued to text him all evening, and in between, I would try to call, but all my calls would go to voicemail.

Was this seriously all about me having one lunch with my coworkers, or did I say something that came out wrong that he got mad at me for? Did his phone just die, and I was freaking out about nothing? I honestly had no idea what was going on, but I truly felt like I didn't exist in his life at that moment. I became a basket case; I was in complete panic mode.

What did I do that made him so mad? Is he done and breaking up with me? Is he having second thoughts about the wedding and spending the rest of his life with me?

"Jonathan, are you breaking off the engagement?"

"Please answer, talk to me. I am at a loss. What happened that made you so mad?"

"I am so sorry. Please, I promise I won't go out with the guys anymore."

"Where are you? Please just answer."

"Don't end things with me like this."

Thoughts kept rushing into my head making it impossible to focus on work or home. It was about twenty-four hours of silent torture when Jonathan texted back. It was one text.

"I will text you in the morning. I am busy."

That night I couldn't sleep. I lay on my side hugging my pillow as a million thoughts continued to circle my brain. Was this just Jonathan's way of dealing with things? Why was I feeling like I had to suck up to him to get his approval again? Why was I losing my mind over him not texting me? I felt like my world was collapsing. We were supposed to be in this together and to enjoy each other and I did not want to be causing him more stress. But I somehow began to wonder why I was always at fault. What did I keep doing wrong? Was I good enough for him? No, I was overthinking this. I was sure the constant travel and long-distance relationship was stressing him out. I was rough around the edges, and Jonathan was much more refined and educated; we were clashing right now. I had to learn to be more like a lady. I had spent so many years with the blue-collar workers swearing and being one of the guys. Once I learned what he liked, and didn't like, I was positive that I wouldn't keep upsetting him so much. I knew I would make him happy; I needed to be more cautious of when to discuss problems and when to pick my battles.

The next morning, I got a "good morning" text from Jonathan. My eyes lit up and I couldn't stop smiling. I was in my happy place again.

"Good morning, Jonathan. I missed you so much," I texted back.

"I was thinking, Kate, why don't you and the girls come up to Chicago this weekend with me? It will be nice to have you come to my place. What do you think?"

"That would be great, hun. It sounds like fun," I answered. I was on cloud nine knowing he was no longer upset with me and we could move forward. That week we talked about when we would drive up and how the girls would react to his house. We hadn't introduced the girls to the place where we would be living one day, and it was time now that they knew we would soon be a family. I still wanted to discuss why he had gotten so mad at me the other night, but I didn't like having deep conversations through text despite my frantic text attempts to know why Jonathan fell off the map. At the end of that week, Jonathan and I met at my house Friday after work. I had already packed the girls a weekend bag and asked my mom to make sure they had eaten dinner early since we didn't want to stop and eat fast food. Detroit to Chicago was about a four-and-a-half-hour drive. The girls did fantastic in the car. I had packed them a travel bag full of snacks and car games. Jonathan and I didn't really talk much on the drive, but we held hands the entire way up. I wasn't very talkative as I was mentally thinking about all the subjects I wanted to mention to him when we had some alone time. I was typically a super chatty person, but when I had stuff on my mind, I became more introverted as I worked thought my different thoughts.

Holding hands was intimate and confirmed that we were still in a good place but needed to find better ways to communicate so that we could resolve issues. I had a particularly hard time with that, with my parents the way they were, and all the screaming I lived through. I tried to avoid topics that would cause confrontation and instead preferred to bottle things up. This was a new relationship and I wanted to make this work so I needed to learn better ways to communicate with Jonathan–one, to better approach him so he wouldn't get mad, and two, to make sure I didn't hold things in.

We pulled into a gated community in Chicago late that evening. The homes were all lakefront properties with small lakes throughout the neighborhood, and every one of them had stylish luxury cars parked out front and a view of the golf course that surrounded the community. Jonathan's place was a huge 3500-square-foot home with a long driveway on half an acre of property. The driveway was lined with solar lights that guided us to the garage. It was all extremely intimidating, especially since we had just left our tiny home in Detroit next to the graffiti-covered stores on the main road of our subdivision.

The girls had fallen asleep on the drive to Chicago the last hour before we pulled into Jonathan's home. When we arrived, we each picked up one of the girls and quietly carried them into the house. I followed

Jonathan in and he escorted me to the spare bedroom where we gently laid them down to sleep. The spare bedroom was bigger than my entire kitchen. It was beautifully furnished with a white, queen-size canopy bed that was centered perfectly against the opposite wall of the main door to the room. There was a plush, white duvet cover on the bed, and as I looked around, I noticed there was no color in the room. It was all very bland and almost reminded me of a hospital. Jonathan smiled and took me by the hand. "Let me show you around, Kate." We walked down the stairs and he began to give me a tour of his beautiful home. The entire home had bamboo floors throughout. The kitchen had beautiful cherry wood cabinets, a breakfast bar, and shiny black granite countertops. The walls were all white throughout the whole house–I wasn't sure if it was because he didn't like color, or he didn't know how to decorate. He only had one single very large black leather sectional in the living room accompanied by an equally large square coffee table. He had an oversized wall-to-wall projection screen TV with surround-sound speakers placed perfectly in the various corners of the living room for the best sound experience. It looked like he had high-quality, expensive furniture, but at the same time the atmosphere was cold and impersonal. It was a beautiful house, but not a home. It didn't feel like a family once lived here with a child. It felt more like a hotel. Would Jonathan be able to adjust to having small kid stuff all over the house again? There were no photos of Scott, wall hangings, or paintings of any sort except one large print of a black panther above the fireplace mantel. The master bedroom, which was on the main floor, had a bathroom with a unique circular shower and an incredibly large oversized hot tub that could easily fit four people. The his and hers walk-in closets were the size of my bedroom in Detroit and were surrounded with cherry wood shelves and built-in compartments and drawers. He didn't have bedroom furniture in the master, which I thought was weird since his spare bedroom clearly was beautifully furnished. I stopped at the mattress and box spring combination and looked up at Jonathan. I was quiet for a moment with a bewildered look on my face.

"Jonathan, what happened to your bedroom furniture? All the other rooms are furnished except for the master." Jonathan looked at me and smiled.

"I got rid of it. I want you to pick something new with me when you move in. The mattress and box spring are brand new, but you must pick the bed frame and matching furniture. I didn't think you wanted to sleep where my ex-wife had once slept," he replied. It was such a considerate gesture. I had never heard of anyone doing that before, and I was excited to pick out bedroom furniture. I had never had bedroom furniture before. I slept on a mattress and box spring at my mom's house because I just never had money to spend on unnecessary luxuries. I walked over to the balcony that was visible through the French doors on the one side of the master. The backyard was hard to see because it was dark out, but my eyes followed the lighting outlining the walkway to what appeared to be a private oasis–a pool with a gazebo and built-in barbecue.

Jonathan could tell I was feeling overwhelmed. I was never quiet. I was fidgeting with my purse strap and looked uneasy. I didn't know where to stand or what to do with myself. My eyes were all over the place as I was trying to take in my surroundings.

"Make yourself at home, Kate. This will all be yours soon when we are married," he said.

But I couldn't get relaxed or comfortable. It was

probably because this was four times the size of my house, or possibly because this was his home originally with his ex and I was a stranger, but whatever the reason, the feeling of uneasiness lingered.

How can I even consider this one day being all mine? I thought to myself.

This was all so grand and so not like how I was used to living. His living room was the size of my entire home. Now I questioned our relationship even more. Why does this man want me? I have nothing to offer. I am seriously nowhere near his level or stature, and there was no way I would fit in.

But Jonathan did his absolute best to welcome us and make us feel comfortable. He had gone shopping during the week to have all our favorite foods and drinks and snacks. He went out of his way to clean out one of the master bedroom's walk-in closets that he had been using as a storage closet so I could hang my clothes to feel more at home.

That evening I showered in his circular shower with a rain showerhead that felt so gentle and relaxing I envisioned myself under a waterfall in a tropical setting. When I got out, Jonathan was patiently waiting while he read his book in bed, giving me quiet time to myself. I came out of the bathroom wearing a long, black silky nightgown with lace around the breasts and a slit up each leg. As I walked, my nightgown flirtatiously exposed my thighs to give him a hint of what was underneath–which was a matching black thong. He patted the bed for me to join him and I slid in beside him. He began to kiss my neck and worked his way down to explore what was under my nightgown, and within seconds, my arousal grew.

"Tell me you want me, Kate," he demanded as he began to kiss me. My heart rate suddenly increased as the tension in my body built up.

I screamed, "Yes, I want you. I want you now!" as I clenched the bed sheets. It didn't take long for me to orgasm as I found my back arching and my toes curling. My lips parted and I screamed with pleasure. My body then froze, and I collapsed into the bed sheets with a smile on my face.

"That was quick!" He smirked.

He climbed on top and I could see his muscles in his arms flex as he held his upper body up and pressed his lower abdomen into mine. I felt his body hit his sexual peak as I told him how I wanted it harder. We both rolled over into the warm down comforter and he spooned me.

"Sleep well. You will need your energy when I wake up and fuck you in the morning," Jonathan said.

Sex became an expectation when we were together. Jonathan claimed he needed it to function. If I declined it, he would get incredibly angry and I would get the silent treatment every time.

Sunday morning, I heard the girls talking downstairs about how amazing Jonathan's house was and how awesome it would be to live here.

"This house is huge. Do you think it's a mansion?" asked Sofia.

"Duh! Look, there is a pool in the backyard!" yelled Hailey.

"Yippee! I want to swim in that right now," replied Sofia.

I got dressed, headed out of the bedroom, and joined them in the kitchen to see what they were hungry for. Jonathan was a light sleeper and felt me get out of bed. He got dressed himself and was not too far behind me.

"Well, girls, what do you think of the place?" he asked as he walked over to give them each a hug.

"Are you hungry for breakfast? We have to head back, but if you want, you can go for a swim in the pool after breakfast before I take you home this afternoon," he offered.

"Hooray!" they yelled, jumping for joy.

"Mom, we don't want to go home. Can we live here?" asked the girls at the same time.

I smiled. "No, girls, we can't stay, but I am so happy you like it here," I told them.

They both frowned and sighed as they walked over to the kitchen table to get ready for breakfast. The girls were in heaven at Jonathan's house. After breakfast they ran around, and I could hear them discussing which room they wanted for their own. It was so cute to hear them happy. I kept hearing one say to the other, "Come look at this," and "Wow, look how big this room is!"

I looked at Jonathan and smiled. "I think the girls are impressed with your house."

He replied, "Of course they are!" Jonathan yelled up in the direction of the girls' voices, "Hey girls, want to go swimming now?" They came running down the stairs both giggling and screaming.

"Yes, please! Mom, can we go now?" I loved seeing smiles on their faces.

"Yes, go upstairs and get your bathing suits on."

"Hurray!" they both said, jumping up and down and then twirling around in circles.

"All right then, go get dressed and bring down a towel each," I said, laughing at their silliness.

Sofia and Hailey ran upstairs, and in lightning speed, they were both back down wearing their bathing suits and ready to go to the pool. I followed them to watch them swim. Jonathan came out with two coffees and stood next to me where I was standing watching the girls.

"Why don't we watch them in the gazebo," he suggested.

"I want to keep an eye on the girls."

"Don't worry, you can see everything from there," he said, gesturing for us to head over.

We walked together holding hands, each with a coffee, toward his gazebo, which was surrounded by glass and had wicker furniture with red cushions and decorative pillows neatly placed and puffed. We sat down beside each other. I leaned over to put down my coffee cup and suddenly felt Jonathan behind me pressing himself against me.

"Jonathan, not here. I need to watch the girls," I replied as I pushed him back.

"Fine, you watch the girls; we both don't need to. Come here, I want my playtime too. You know you can't say no to me, Kate. I know you want me to fuck you right here," he said. He placed his left hand inside my panties and his right hand under my shirt and clenched my breast.

"You are mine," he said, then he pulled his arm out from under my shirt, pulled his pants down, and pulled up my skirt.

"Seriously, Jonathan, the girls are going to see you," I said, squirming to push him back.

"Stop fighting it. I want you, Kate. Mmm, you feel so good," he said as he nibbled my ear. While standing behind me, he pushed himself inside. I didn't know what to do. I kept my eyes locked on the girls but deep down I wanted him to continue.

"Kate, I need you." Within a few minutes, he released me, pulled his pants back up, and grabbed his coffee. He had his orgasm but left me wanting more.

"Now you are all over me and I am swimming inside you. It's the way I like it. I get to leave you wanting more and I feel like I can conquer the world. Tonight, I will make love to you but for now, I must go finish up a few things before we go. I will meet you inside when the girls are done." He kissed me on my forehead, leaving me standing there with my jaw wide open, shaking my head.

What was that? I thought. Jonathan is very spontaneous sexually, but that was a little too far. I couldn't believe he had just done that. *He doesn't own my body. I am not that beautiful that he can't control his sexual urges, and what if the girls had seen?* Did he feel entitled to my body now that we were engaged? In fact, there was nothing romantic about what he had just done. It wasn't romantic, but it was kind of thrilling and exhilarating. I did say *not now*, but him wanting me so intensely was very arousing. *Should I be worried I am getting married to a sex addict? Should I be worried that I was aroused by that? No, he can't be a sex addict; it's not like we are constantly having sex every hour of the day. I will talk to him later. For now, I will just let the girls have their moment.*

CHAPTER SEVEN
LASTING IMPRESSIONS

SUNDAY, AFTER THE GIRLS FINISHED THEIR SWIM, we packed up and Jonathan drove us back home. It was a quiet ride home; the girls were each entertained with their travel activity kits, and I was upset with Jonathan and his inappropriate and unexpected sex in the gazebo. All I could think about was whether I should be concerned about his behavior or whether I should be flattered he thinks I am that desirable. *Why don't I know what to think?* I was rolling around so many thoughts in my head from this weekend; I was quietly staring out the window for most of the drive.

"Everything okay, Kate?" Jonathan asked a few different times throughout the drive, and my response was always, "I'm good, thanks." I needed to talk to him. Jonathan had been with me long enough to know I always got really quiet when I was either depressed or upset–I was an open book of emotions. When we got back to Detroit, it was midafternoon, and the girls rushed into the house to see their grandma and tell her all about the trip. I held back with Jonathan to talk to him about what happened in the gazebo.

"Jonathan, what was that all about at the pool this morning? I didn't expect you to just take me like that in broad daylight. Don't you think it was inappropriate? I mean, the girls weren't far–what if they had seen us?" I asked.

I wasn't happy with him and my irritation was clear in my tone and attitude that I was giving him, and when I wanted to talk about it, he just belittled my concerns and laughed. "Come on, Kate, you need to learn to be more fun and spontaneous. I obviously knew exactly where the girls were, and they couldn't see us." He smirked as if there was no reason for me to overreact. "Anyway, I thought you liked being naughty. When did you get all serious? You need to enjoy the moment and have fun. Honestly, Kate, we need to take advantage of the free moments we get–we don't get many," he said as he grabbed our luggage out of the trunk and headed toward the house.

"I'm not uptight and that was too risky, Jonathan," I answered back, but it didn't really make much of a difference since he was already headed into the house and I was arguing with the back of his head. He didn't turn his head to acknowledge my reply, which made me even more annoyed.

I don't want the girls or my mom to know what's going on, so I will pretend for now and we can continue this when the kids go to sleep, I thought as I slammed closed the trunk of the car and stormed inside.

It was Hailey and Sofia's first road trip anywhere and Jonathan's house was like a resort for them, and I didn't want to ruin it by starting a fight with Jonathan. Not to mention, it was not a topic for little girls' ears. They were way too young to hear us talking about where we should and should not have sex. I let it go for the short time being, but I had full intentions to continue talking about his thrill-seeking sex and why I didn't appreciate him laughing at me.

Jonathan had dinner with us and stayed overnight. He played princess and dragon with Hailey and Sofia, pretending the playscape was a castle and he was the mean dragon that would eat the princesses if he caught them. The girls ran around laughing and running from the dragon. I was overly impressed by him as a future stepdad. There was nothing more attractive than a man who was nurturing and valued family. It was everything I ever dreamed a good lifelong partner would be, and the girls loved him. It was the girls' bedtime, so I sent them to get ready, and Jonathan, my mom, and I headed over to the table for a drink and some conversation.

"Jonathan, you are so good with children. I am sure your son adores you!" commented my mom.

"Oh, thank you, Beth. The girls are so precious. You have beautiful grandchildren. You should be proud," replied Jonathan, charming my mother, but surprisingly I noticed he didn't make any mention about Scott to her when she commented on his son. Mom wasn't one to be patient and, not giving him a chance to further engage in the conversation, she immediately continued her hosting duties that she missed doing because we never had guests over.

"Would you like a drink, Jonathan?" asked my mother.

"Just a water would be wonderful, Beth. Thank you. Have I told you I now see where Kate gets her beauty and grace from?" Jonathan replied. My mom blushed and giggled.

"You have and you are too kind. Thank you, Jonathan." We sat around and talked for a little longer when Sofia came over to the table.

“We are ready, Mommy,” she exclaimed, still excited from all the play earlier.

“Okay, come on, little girl, let’s get you into bed,” I told her as I reached for her hand. I stood up from the table. “I’m going to put the girls to bed,” I said. Jonathan grabbed my arm and kissed my hand.

“Hurry back, sweetie, and know you are loved,” he said ever-so sweetly. My mom smiled at us both, delighted we had found each other.

My mom thought Jonathan was a keeper, thinking he was someone special that would be awesome for me and the girls. *What’s not to love*, she would tell me; he was smart and successful, and he would provide a good life for the girls and me. How could I talk to her about what I was feeling and my doubts? She would think I was trying to find reasons to ruin something good. I left them to keep chatting while I followed the girls upstairs to tuck them into bed. I kissed Hailey and went to lie beside Sofia until she fell asleep. Sofia didn’t like going to bed by herself and no matter how tired she was, the darkness would keep her awake at night. She always worried about monsters in her closet and even with the nightlight I had put in her room, she still wouldn’t go to sleep alone. That night I ended up falling asleep beside her in her bed by mistake. After my long days, I would close my eyes waiting for Sofia to fall asleep and I would find myself waking up to my morning alarm to repeat the day. This time was different. I woke up to the scary feeling that someone was watching me. I instantly opened my eyes to see it was Jonathan standing over me glaring at me. His face was serious. He had a look about him that parents gave their child when they did something wrong and were in trouble. It was an unsettling look. He turned and stormed out of the girls’ room. He was upset, and he stormed off to sit on the couch in my living room. I jumped up from Sofia's bed and went after him, still trying to wake up after falling asleep with Sofia for what seemed to be only five minutes. I sat down beside him, and he instantly gave me the cold shoulder.

"What do you think you are doing, Katelyn? Do you always fall asleep with your kids and leave your boyfriend hanging for an hour by himself?" he asked in a detached and uncaring way. Whenever Jonathan was upset with me, he would drop all the cute pet names and go straight for my full name to show he was disappointed.

"I drove all this way to be with you and stay overnight, and this is how you show your appreciation?" he asked.

"What, I was asleep for an hour. I am so sorry, Jonathan," I pleaded. I couldn't believe I had completely passed out and left him all by himself with my mother. I was so embarrassed and in disbelief I had done that. "I didn't mean to fall asleep; I closed my eyes for a second. I was just really tired from the drive."

Jonathan folded his arms and refused to give me any type of acknowledgement. My mom came into the room to wish us both good night, and Jonathan instantly shifted his demeanor 180 degrees and was charming, even getting up to hug her good night. I could feel the tension between us, but he was very skilled at masking his emotions around others. My mom certainly had no clue that Jonathan was upset, never mind that I was getting the cold shoulder at that moment. She was just passing by and too tired to detect the tension in the air. My mom was so taken with how polite and charming he was, she didn't notice the almost bipolar mood swings that I was beginning to see but not understand. To the outside world he was always polite and respectful, but eventually he would reveal his true self. He wouldn't let many people see that side of him, protecting his true personality so that only the few that were in his deep circle saw it.

My mother said good night to us, and Jonathan almost instantly turned detached and withdrawn again, and reverted to being virtually childish in his behavior. He got all serious and crossed his arms across his chest, making deep sighs of disappointment, while slightly turning his body away from me to distance himself as he pouted.

And it was working. It was very selfish of me and I felt guilty for not being considerate that he was a visitor who I had left stranded. I apologized to him multiple times while I placed my hand on his shoulder and tried to turn him so he would look at me. I rubbed and kissed his back and slowly snaked my hands under his shirt where I made my way to his chest. My finger trailed over his nipple and I continued until he finally forgave me. He was acting a bit dramatic at the whole sleeping thing. I thought, *it's not like it is the worst thing in the world. So, I fell asleep.* I didn't say it out loud, but I thought he was behaving like a bit of a baby.

"Well, Kate, you know how you can make it up to me," he said while he undressed me with his eyes.

There was no question how I could make it up to him. Jonathan took me by the hand and led me upstairs to my bedroom, shut the door, and I began to make it up to him. I wasn't in the mood, so I pleased him and then I faked it. With everything that had happened today, I couldn't get aroused at all and I wasn't going to continue the fight; it was just easier to fake it and move on. I ended up lying in bed for hours that night. We didn't get a chance to finish our conversation about the gazebo sex, and on top of that, I ended up apologizing for being tired. It was not the way I had expected this weekend to go. I was overthinking it, but I felt that every apology I gave seemed to take him longer to accept. Like he was punishing me for making errors, and maybe I was wrong, but I was beginning to think that he liked it when he made me grovel, like it turned him on because we always seemed to have make-up sex. Jonathan woke up in the middle of the night and saw I was awake.

"It's one in the morning, sweetheart. Are you okay? I don't like it when we fight either," he whispered and hugged me tight. "This is where you belong–in my arms forever. Try to get some sleep."

Around four-thirty in the morning I felt Jonathan's hand on my breast. It was awfully early in the morning, and I hadn't gotten much sleep, so I wasn't awake, but it felt nice having a man reach for me.

He pulled me in closer toward him and with his hand on one breast, he reached for his penis with the other and he slipped in and began to have sex with me. I was slowly just waking up. My forehead wrinkled and eyes squinted as I was caught by surprise. Was he having sex with me while I was sleeping? I had never experienced a man having sleepy sex with me before. He pushed hard for a short while, pressing his hand into my pelvis to get the feeling of being in deep, while squeezing my breast and pulling at my nipple repeatedly. I felt his body tense inside of me as he finished. It was quick and then he fell back asleep, leaving me scratching my head about what had just happened. It was very selfish on his part to meet his needs and go back to sleep. What about me? I was happy he had enjoyed himself, but isn't it better when both of us are engaged? I didn't understand. Was he even awake? Our alarm went off at five in the morning. That night went way too fast and I woke up feeling extremely tired. I was groggy, I couldn't seem to open my eyes fully, and I had a mild headache.

We both showered and dressed, and during coffee, I asked him about his morning sex.

"I absolutely love sleepy sex. It's a whole new feeling when we are both completely in a relaxed state and we can join our bodies," he said to me. "Knowing I am leaving but I'm still inside of you feels amazing."

I had never thought of it that way. Sleepy sex–was that a new thing? Had I been out of the dating scene so long that I had missed out on all the sex trends? This one seemed a bit odd as it clearly only satisfied him, but it seemed to excite him knowing he came inside of me, almost like he was marking his territory. If that put his mind at ease while he was traveling the whole week, who was I to question his need for intimacy? Didn't all men want to be intimate with their partner?

He had told me his reasons for liking sleepy sex; I just was not sure if I should've felt flattered or conquered. I did enjoy his touch, but when I became fully conscious, I was left with the feeling that fulfilling his needs was an expectation of the relationship. Every man wanted to be close with the woman they loved. In actuality, he was just a man that wanted to be with his woman before he left her for the week. Sleepy sex was his way to feel me one more time before he was gone. Anyway, no one could keep that rhythm for long; it would die down when he got to be with me every night as husband and wife. Or so I thought.

CHAPTER EIGHT
Gown Shopping Gone Wrong

I WAS STILL BLOWN AWAY THAT I WAS ENGAGED AND would soon be calling Jonathan my husband. We spent the next month and a half trying to plan our wedding. We both agreed, since it was the second wedding for the both of us, a destination wedding-honeymoon was the perfect way to go. It didn't make sense to spend tons of money the second time, plus both of us had hectic work-home schedules, so we wanted to do something simple for just the two of us. The plan was to throw a big reception party when we got back home so that our families could celebrate with us. When Jonathan traveled and stayed in Michigan, we would stay up on our laptops searching destination wedding locations.

"Okay, Kate, where do you want to stay? We need to pick a location for our wedding soon."

"I don't really know, babe. You are the world traveler–what do you suggest? I don't want to go far because the kids are so small. Can we stay within a three- or four-hour flight just in case?"

"Well, that limits our choices."

"Really? Aren't the islands close?" I asked. "How about

the Bahamas?" I said, excited. I had never been to any of the Caribbean Islands.

He vetoed my first suggestion. "No, it's not that warm this time of the year."

"Okay, how about Jamaica?"

"No, I don't like the food," he said, shooting down my second recommendation.

"Okay, how about Haiti?"

"No, I don't think it's very safe there," he replied, dismissing my third suggestion.

"Fine, how about you suggest a destination? I will be content with any of them and you are more familiar with the different places since you've traveled all over the world," I said, wanting to stop offering my ideas since I kept getting rejected without any hesitation on his part.

This lasted every night for a full month as we tried to find the perfect destination wedding, and I would end up getting sleepy every time, which would end the search. Our evenings became somewhat like Groundhog Day. I was getting tired of looking, and it felt like we would never get to our destination wedding. I was very flexible on where we should go. Frankly, if there was sun and sand and beaches, I was more than pleased, but Jonathan was not as flexible. He was an over-achiever and tended to be a perfectionist, making sure everything was flawless. Unfortunately, attention to detail was not a skill of mine. I just wanted a tropical getaway to say "I do" with the intentions of spending the rest of the trip on the beach drinking piña coladas. We finally settled on Mexico. Jonathan was fluent in five languages including Spanish, so getting around would not be an issue–that's if we left the room at all. He had two masters' degrees in business and electrical engineering and had traveled and lived all around the world for work. Every country he spent time in he would hire private tutors to teach him the native language of the country. He went to Germany, Mexico, China, France and England. Mexico had luxury five-star hotels, and since he had lived in Mexico for an international assignment, he settled on that as our wedding-honeymoon spot.

The next thing we had to choose was a hotel and, specifically, a room. There were so many choices. King bed with ocean view, oceanfront, garden view–the list went on with some of these places. I was happy with any hotel, and the room wasn't something I was focused on. I personally was just ecstatic to leave Michigan for a week and be at the beach. It was February, and Michigan winters were fierce. Typical temperatures were around twenty degrees Fahrenheit, and everything was covered with snowfall that ranged between one to twelve inches multiple days of the week. All I cared about was having an adventure and enjoying someone else's cooking for a week.

Jonathan, on the other hand, was conditioned to expect certain amenities and had specifics he required for considering a hotel. The hotel had to be five-star luxury and had to have at least three gourmet restaurants. The room had to have a king-size bed with a 180-degree unspoiled oceanfront view. Jonathan was willing to pay dearly for his view. He said the view of the ocean was the only thing that "recharged his batteries." The hotel had to have multiple spa treatments on the resort, accessible at any hour, and it had to have excellent office capabilities in case he had to plug in for work.

Jonathan was on call 24/7 for the company and was required to answer any time they needed to bring him in. He was very business minded and having the ability to make sure he was reachable was a priority. I was irritated about this and brought it up.

"Jonathan, why do you have to bring your laptop? You always tell me no electronics when we are together."

"Kate, I'm sorry but work is work, and I can't be vice president if I am not reachable 24/7. Plus, everyone knows I am on vacation. I am sure I won't be online much if at all."

Jonathan looked at every room at every luxury resort in Mexico. Just like when we argued over where to go for our wedding, picking a room was just as frustrating for me.

One night we were looking for hours and everything I suggested was completely dismissed.

"Oh, Jonathan, this room is beautiful. Look at this one. Let's pick this," I said, shifting my laptop toward him.

"Let me see," he said, scrolling down to the descriptions of the room and hotel.

"No, Kate, this one only has one restaurant. We need at least three to choose from or we will get bored with the food."

"All right," I said, taking back my computer while slightly annoyed at his nitpicking.

I continued researching and found another possibility and turned my computer to show Jonathan once again.

"Okay, this one is definitely a good one."

"Are you crazy? This is only a three-star hotel. We can't stay in that. Focus on four- or five-star only please," he replied, once again finding fault with my choice.

Again, I continued to research and found one that I absolutely loved. It hit all his requirements from what I thought. Five-star hotel and four restaurants to choose from: Italian, Chinese, Mexican, and a steakhouse, plus buffet and à la carte. Although, I knew from our previous vacation that he wouldn't eat at a buffet, so it didn't qualify.

"Okay, this one is perfect. Look at this one. Let's book it," I said, excited I had finally found a room and we could move on from this continuous, relentless research.

"Absolutely no way. This is ocean view. I only book oceanfront," Jonathan said, criticizing what I didn't understand.

"That's the same thing," I replied.

"No, hun, please just trust me. Ocean view is a view from a distance. I need oceanfront so I can sit and enjoy the ocean right from my balcony with nothing in my way. I am not flying all that way and spending all this money to not have the ocean at my doorstep," he replied with a hint of insult that I had even questioned him.

I really was exhausted going through each room in such detail. I was more of a shoot-by-the-hip kind of girl, so these long nights of research to find the perfect spot was mentally exhausting for me. It was becoming so much that I ended up falling asleep. Jonathan got upset one night and questioned my interest.

"Kate, wake up, are you actually interested in this wedding? Because I feel like I am the one doing all the work here," he snapped at me after he had shaken me awake. "You obviously don't care about our wedding, or am I that boring?" He frowned.

I didn't understand why he was so upset. Maybe it was because he was trying so hard to make sure everything was perfect for us and I was not putting in an equivalent effort to help.

He closed his computer and rolled over, giving me the

cold shoulder.

Ugh, what did I do now? I thought as I shook off my sleepiness.

"Jonathan, what did I do? I just dozed off for a second. Don't be mad again. Come on." I shook his shoulder, trying to force him to turn toward me.

"Please, turn around and look at me. I'm sorry I dozed off. I am only tired from my long days. I love you very much and can't wait to be your wife," I cried as I kissed the back of his shoulder, trying to get him to face me. I felt like I was groveling for his attention and forgiveness—again. It was my fault he was angry tonight; I fell asleep on him for a second time, and I appeared uninterested in helping him find a vacation spot. I shouldn't expect him to do all the work, but he is the researcher and the one who has specific requirements for his vacation. If it's a five-star hotel, I was happy. But that wasn't what Jonathan wanted to see. I had to try harder to do my part in our wedding planning even if every suggestion I made was turned down and we ended up picking what he wanted anyway. Jonathan finally felt I had enough silent treatment for the night and was interested in moving on to having make-up sex. That seemed to be our thing. He would get mad at me, I would apologize, and then we would have make-up sex, or I would get mad, he would defend himself, I would apologize for overreacting, and then we would have make-up sex. It all ended with make-up sex. I don't know if fights were supposed to create passion, so make-up sex was important to blow off steam, but I personally wasn't good at make-up sex. I lacked the ability to easily switch to becoming sexually aroused right after having a heated argument. It was too much of an emotional roller coaster.

Jonathan finally settled on a location and a hotel

room he was satisfied with and purchased our tickets to Mexico. He planned for us to depart in May. I had three months to find a wedding dress. It was moving so fast. I mentioned how quickly we were moving to Jonathan, and he snapped back.

"Kate, do you really expect me to be traveling this much our whole lives? I can't be driving back and forth and staying at your house all the time. I have responsibilities at my home, and I have a son I need to be with as well. It's time you joined me there so we can be together in one place," he said with a harsh and intimidating edge as he made sure I understood the sacrifices he was making for me.

I guess he made sense. In fact, I really couldn't complain. Jonathan was the one doing all the driving to see me. He was very dedicated to our relationship, so for me to ask him to keep traveling to see me was a bit unreasonable. Long-distance relationships didn't work, and we had been doing it for a considerable amount of time and he was reaching his limit. He was ready to have me by his side as his wife.

Jonathan was going to be in Chicago for the next month so we would only be talking at night during the week and we would see each other on weekends. Jonathan would drive down Friday night after work and then go back to Chicago Monday at the crack of dawn to be back in the office. I had never met someone so determined to be with me. I guess it's true–if a man loves you, he will do anything to be with you. I felt so special knowing he was investing so much effort to be with me. But of course, that also meant four o'clock in the morning sleepy sex.

I didn't complain because he left with a smile on his face and I knew he was thinking of me. He said he loved the idea of coming inside of me before he left for the week. The idea of leaving with his cum still inside me gave him pleasure.

Was I becoming his territory in his mind? I did like giving him something to remember me by when he left, and I loved the fact that he woke me up to make love. I, on the other hand, was not sure about him having sex with me while I was not fully awake and finishing before I had the chance to completely wake up to enjoy it myself before he was back asleep and snoring.

The three months were flying by and I finally found the dress I was in love with in a magazine. I called around multiple bridal shops in Detroit and came across a boutique that had the dress on the shelf. I booked a morning appointment that weekend to see the dress. Jonathan was staying in Chicago with Scott, so I made plans to go with my mom and the girls to the boutique. It was going to be a perfect fun girls' day out, with dress shopping, lunch, and then a movie.

When we arrived at the boutique, the lady handed me the dress she had reserved for me to try on. She led us to a private room where there was a comfy couch for my mom and the girls to wait on while I went into the changing room to try on the dress. I came out of the dressing room and the girls' eyes lit up.

"Wow, Mom, you look so beautiful!" said Hailey.

"Yes, dear, you really do make a stunning bride," said my mom as she came over to see the dress up close.

I walked over to Sofia and kneeled in front of her. "What do you think, Sofia? Do you like the dress?"

"Yes, Mama, it's very pretty," she said with her soft, sweet voice.

I kissed her on the forehead, stood up, looked at the sales lady that was helping us, and said, "I will take it."

I was so excited I had found my dress, I had to call

Jonathan to tell him.

He texted me back. “Can I call you later?”

“No problem, call me when you get home.”

I spent the rest of the day with my mom and the girls. The girls loved Disney movies and princesses, and *Frozen II* had just come out so it was a great opportunity to use up the gift card that Jonathan gave me to the movie theater. That evening after I settled the girls and got them to sleep, I called Jonathan to tell him all about our day. He listened until the point when I told him what my mom and the girls thought about the dress I picked.

“Wait, you went with your mom and the girls to try on your wedding dress? You mean they have already seen the dress you are going to wear for the wedding?” he asked.

“Yes, what’s wrong with that? They loved it and said I look beautiful.”

Jonathan suddenly got quiet and I could feel the tension through the phone instantly. *Why is he annoyed about this? It’s a good thing*, I thought.

“Kate, I didn’t want anyone to see you in your dress first. I am the one who is supposed to see you in your dress first. That was supposed to be a private thing, not for your children and mother!”

I could feel the cold shoulder through the phone.

“I don’t think this is something you should be upset about. It felt wonderful being able to share this with them. Why are you making such a big deal about this?” I replied as I began to defend myself, but I could already see it wasn’t going to end well.

“No, if you can’t see that this is something special that we should be sharing for just the both of us, then obviously this doesn't mean as much to you as it does to me," he said. "I am investing all this time and money to be with you and the least you could do is show some appreciation and respect our privacy."

"I'm sorry, Jonathan, I do appreciate everything you do for me and I do value our relationship. I didn't see the big deal in sharing this moment with my kids and mom," I said with a soft and disappointed voice.

I was expecting to have a happy conversation, as all I wanted to do was share my day with my soon-to-be husband, but it ended up with me feeling awful and disheartened.

"Are you trying to make this day about us or about everyone else?" he spoke into the phone with a cold, irritable tone.

"No, I am not trying to make this day about everyone else. I'm so sorry; I didn't mean to upset you and make you think I didn't appreciate you. I was just excited and wanted to share it with mom and the girls, especially since they won't be at the ceremony." I burst into tears. "Jonathan, please don't be angry with me. I love you. I was simply happy I found my dress."

I didn't know why I was apologizing other than I knew he felt let down, and I didn't want our wedding and the thought of our marriage to be negative in any way.

"Okay, Kate, I forgive you. Just understand we don't get a lot of time together, and this is the second marriage for both of us. I want it to be about us, and only us. Do you understand?" he explained, giving me his reasons for his disapproval of my day.

"Yes, I understand. I know we don't get a lot of time, and I wasn't trying to do anything wrong."

I was crushed. I had been so happy all day, so delighted to find the right dress that I would look beautiful in. I was in such high spirits, and after sharing the news with Jonathan, I ended up feeling guilty that I had shared my special moment with my mom, Sofia, and Hailey. I didn't ask Jonathan if this was something he wanted to participate in, and instead, I took it upon myself to assume he didn't, and it only caused friction between us. When I told my mother I had found the dress, she began to cry that she was so happy for me. How could I tell her now that Jonathan was angry that she had seen the dress before him? I wanted my mom to be proud. I couldn't bring her into our fights because then we would make up and I would leave her with unresolved feelings toward him. No, I wouldn't mention this to Mom.

CHAPTER NINE

For Better or Worse

IN NO TIME, JONATHAN AND I WERE GETTING READY to head off to Mexico. We stayed in a hotel near the airport the night before because our flight was so early in the morning. I had bought so much stuff for this trip, especially a very sexy bikini that I was dying to wear for him. He hadn't seen me in a bikini yet; for our last trip I had only worn a one-piece.

The next morning, we headed out to Mexico. It wasn't a long flight–about three hours–but by the time we spent before leaving Detroit to board and the time we spent in Mexico after we arrived, it was a full day of travel. We were greeted by a very friendly shuttle bus driver sent by the hotel. He welcomed us with a smile that felt genuine and kind. He helped us with our luggage and drove us to a large Greyhound-style bus. The hotels hire this service to bring their guests to the hotel from the airport.

"Where are the beautiful couple traveling from?" the bus driver asked with broken English.

"Michigan," I replied.

"Oh, it is cold in Michigan, no?" he asked.

"*Sí, señor,*" I responded, feeling pleased with myself for replying in Spanish.

We arrived at the resort around 3:30 p.m. The hotel staff presented each guest with a mimosa and a hot face cloth. They escorted us to an air-conditioned lobby while we waited for them to check us in. The room was decorated with chic wicker furniture, a stucco ceiling, chandeliers, and oversized windows with a view of the ocean. A fresh grapefruit aroma lingered throughout the guest waiting room.

Jonathan and I waited while the resort staff checked in each couple, one at a time. I was really in no rush as I was taking in all the luxuries that the hotel had to offer in just this one spot, but I could see Jonathan was getting restless. He was fidgeting, constantly checking his watch and huffing with frustration that he was expected to wait this long to get a room. He had a bit of an expectation that he was entitled to being taken care of in a timely matter due to how much he was paying, but there was no rushing here.

"Would you please relax," I said, holding his knee down to stop him from bouncing his leg. "Just enjoy your drink. We're here together, that's all that matters."

"Yeah, right. I will enjoy myself when I am finally in my hotel room–that's what matters," Jonathan muttered, displeased.

The staff called us up to check in and ordered a bellboy to help us with our luggage. We were escorted by the bellboy through the hotel where he gave us the rundown of the different restaurants, activities, pool locations, and finally to our room to get settled in. Jonathan gave me a five-dollar US bill to tip the bellboy. I didn't understand why because I felt it was something he should have done. *Maybe I'm just an old-fashioned type of girl, but I just feel tipping is something for the man to take care of–especially when we are on vacation and together. But whatever, it's fine*, I thought.

As soon as we were alone, Jonathan grabbed me by my waist and began to take my clothes off. The type of sex where the chemistry is so intense your heart races with every second. The type of intimacy that makes me want to taste him with passionate kisses while running our hands all over each other. Jonathan brought me to the bed, picked me up, and dropped me down, kneeling in front of me. I knew this was the beginning of what would be an amazing and relaxing vacation. He knew exactly how I liked it. I froze, clenched the sheets, and released.

"Oh, Jonathan!" I screamed with pleasure.

He stood up, pulled his pants down, climbed on top of my limp body, and took his turn. When he climaxed, he rolled over and squeezed me tight to cuddle with him.

"Nap time," he said.

"What, are you joking? I don't want to nap; I want to check the place out," I said, surprised that he really was serious about taking a nap.

"We will as soon as we take a small nap, baby," he said. "Come on, curl up beside me. You know I don't rest well unless I can feel your body next to mine." He spoke in a soft but almost commanding way. How could I say no to a sweet request as to him wanting to cuddle? After all, the reason we were there was to enjoy each other's company.

I wasn't at all tired, but I obliged. He was being sweet and lovable, and I wasn't there to argue. Plus, after the go-go-go that had been my life, it wasn't a bad suggestion to just chill for a bit. *I will get up when he falls asleep*, I thought as I made plans in my head what I wanted to see first at the resort. But unfortunately, after waking up super early to drive to the airport and flying all day, I ended up drifting off. I woke up at seven that evening starving and annoyed that we wasted the first day of our trip sleeping.

"Calm down, Kate. Don't worry, we will check the hotel out in the morning," he said as he grabbed the key card to our room to get ready to head out for dinner.

I took a deep breath. I was calm, but I didn't like that I had wasted an entire day sleeping. I never got to travel like Jonathan did.

Relax, Kate, this trip is about spending time together, not about the quantity of things we see and do, I thought.

I closed my eyes, took a deep breath, and released a mindful sigh before walking toward Jonathan. We were headed to the steakhouse restaurant on the opposite end of the resort and approached the front desk host. Jonathan asked for a booth for two.

The host asked for our name and room number. "Sir, I do not see your name here. Did you make a reservation?" he asked politely.

"Reservation?" Jonathan turned and looked at me. "Kate, didn't you call for reservations?" he asked, irritated. "They told us to do that as soon as we got to our room."

"No, we fell asleep, remember?" I replied with a hint of sarcasm, but he squinted his eyes at me unappreciative of my attempt to add humor to my response. I reached for him and countered my response with an apology and explanation. "Jonathan, I really am sorry. I didn't think about it after we got into our room and got busy. I will fix it."

Jonathan turned away from me and stormed off toward our room. The maître d' frowned and looked at me like he was sorry that I was having to deal with a full-grown man having a meltdown. I thanked him and ran after Jonathan in my three-inch heels, which I had worn to impress him. I grabbed Jonathan's hand and stopped him.

"I'm sorry. I didn't know you expected me to make the reservations. I will fix it in the morning. Let's go to the buffet and get something to eat for tonight. I am totally okay with that," I pleaded.

"Are you serious? I don't do buffets," he said.

He snatched his hand back and kept walking, leaving me looking foolish and alone in front of one of the many beautiful courtyards within the hotel. A wave of loneliness nearly knocked me over, and I was left wondering what had just happened. In less than twenty-four hours I would be saying vows to the same man that just became upset with me for an unclear expectation. I walked over to the buffet, grabbed a to-go plate, and headed to a lounge chair on the beach, eating my dinner alone under the stars while watching the waves crash onto the shore. *How is this normal*, I thought as I gazed upon a couple strolling on the beach holding hands and laughing while enjoying each other's company. *Should I marry Jonathan? Why are we not like that couple? Is it me? What am I doing wrong? Why can't I get anything right? It feels like if we aren't having sex, we are arguing about something and I am making mistakes that make him angry. I wish my mom and the girls were here, so I wasn't alone.* I felt unsettled, confused, and lonesome. *Maybe it's not me at all. Maybe he is feeling stressed about the wedding, his job, the money we are spending,* I began to rationalize in my head. I felt concerned for Jonathan and his inability to express his feelings, but I wasn't going to run away from him because of that. I was there to help him and support him even though I was feeling upset that the night was ruined.

I walked back to our room and found Jonathan reading his book on the patio. He didn't acknowledge me when I walked in and I went straight to the bathroom to shower. I didn't want him to see that I had been crying and upset. What should have been a romantic dinner turned into me eating alone, wondering how I could be better. When I came out, Jonathan was waiting in bed for me to make love. Was he already okay with what happened, and why did he not want to discuss it?

He smiled at me, and when I climbed into bed, he made his move and climbed on top. *Should I stop him? No, let this go. I don't want to spend our only few days here fighting about the little stuff.* I gave into his foreplay and enjoyed what he was so good at. I was still feeling uncomfortable with unresolved blame and how he had brushed me off and left me without a second thought. He had a strange ability to make me feel like I was on an emotional roller coaster–happiness, anger, guilt, anxiety, loneliness, doubt, and arousal all in one night. It was at the end of the night, and he had successfully awakened my sexual peak. His head was under the sheets in between my thighs so I couldn't see him, but oh I could feel every lick and suck. Surprisingly after the extreme emotional ups and downs that day, he still had the ability to help me have a powerful orgasm. Once he had finished me, he climbed on top of me and I lifted my hips, inviting him to take his turn.

The next morning was the morning of our wedding. I had so many mixed feelings running through my head about the night before. *This is the man I will be spending the rest of my life with. I was lucky he chose me*, I thought. *My knight in shining armor. Jonathan is handsome and successful, and he wants me. Every girl like me would be so lucky to be in my shoes.* I just needed to understand all the mixed feelings I was experiencing in our relationship. I got out of bed to find Jonathan sipping his coffee, reading his book on the patio, and facing the crashing waves from the sea in front of our room. It was a breathtaking view, really. Jonathan finished his page he was so focused on and looked up at me.

"Good morning, Kate. Are you ready for breakfast?"

I smiled and nodded. He knew me well. He would always say I had a healthy appetite for a lady with such a tiny frame. I slipped on a cute little red sundress and we headed for the restaurant serving breakfast that morning. We approached the female hostess who asked us for our name and room number. Jonathan replied and quickly followed with his request for a table with an ocean view. One thing was for sure, Jonathan was very particular where he sat at restaurants–usually always a booth or facing the water. I wasn't sure why; I guess everyone had their quirks. Indisputably, booths allowed us to sit beside each other so he could hold my hand or fondle me without anyone noticing. The hostess escorted us to our table and kindly pulled the chair out for me. We both sat down and we each requested a coffee. Then we people-watched in silence. I was still thinking about last night's lack of companionship at dinner and was pondering today's events with the wedding. Jonathan suddenly broke the silence.

"Kate, why don't you go get a massage this morning before our big day? It will help you relax, and then you can get your hair done. Try calling them now to see if they can squeeze you in for an appointment."

It was a thoughtful suggestion; a massage would put my nerves at ease. "I think that's a great idea, sweetheart," I replied.

I reached for my phone. I dialed the number to the front desk and asked them to patch me through to their salon. A lady with a Hispanic accent answered the phone.

"*Hola*, this is Muy Linda Salon, how can I service you?"

"*Hola*, my name is Katelyn from Room 1013. Do you have time this morning for a massage and hair style?"

"Let me look, *señorita*. Yes, I do have a slot in 30 minutes if you can come?" she asked.

"That's perfect, thank you, I will see you then!" And with a big smile I hung up the phone.

"I am assuming by your bright eyes and smile you are getting a massage?"

I nodded but then it struck me. "Wait... What will you do while I am at the spa, hun? Are you sure you're okay if I leave you?" I asked.

"Don't worry about me, Kate. I have a good book to go back to. Go enjoy yourself. You deserve it," he replied as he smiled.

Wow, I thought. *I seriously don't know what I did to deserve such an amazing guy, but I thank my lucky stars for whatever it is.* After breakfast, Jonathan walked me to the spa, gave me a kiss on my lips, and I returned it with a French kiss to make sure he would have something to think about while I was getting pampered. He turned to head off but not before saying, "Have fun, baby. See you when you're done."

I smiled and waved. "Thanks, babe!" Then I entered the luxurious spa.

I was greeted by the aroma of lavender that was wafting through the air. It was instant happiness that I felt. The spa was stunning and almost reminded me of a Greek paradise. There were soaring ceilings with tall columns, marble flooring, and floor-to-ceiling windows. It was very impressive. I walked up to the hostess but not before absorbing it all.

"May I help you, *señorita*?" asked the hostess, a young beauty with dark brown eyes and long, black hair that reached her waist.

"Yes, I have an appointment. Katelyn from room 1013."

"Ah, *sí*, here you are, Mrs. Katelyn," said the hostess. "Please have a seat and your masseuse will be right out."

I walked over to the black leather couches that were in the lobby. I sat down and continued taking in the amazing aroma and incredible architecture and decor. A voice calling my name snapped me out of my trance.

"Mrs. Katelyn, please come with me. I'm your masseuse."

I jumped up and followed her through large wooden mahogany doors into what appeared to be a locker room.

"My name is Maria." Please take all your clothes off including undergarments and put the robe on in the changing room. When you're ready, put all your belongings in the locker outside the changing room. I will wait for you outside."

I thanked her and went to get changed. There was a beautiful, soft white, terrycloth robe in the changing room that smelled of lavender. I proceeded to take off all my clothes and put on the robe. I put all my clothes, flip-flops, and cell phone together–gathering it all into a ball–and walked out of the room to meet Maria. She pointed to the open locker room and I shoved it all in, not the least bit graceful. She closed the door and pulled out the key for me to take.

"Place the elastic band on the key around your wrist so you don't lose it," she suggested.

She led me to the next room, which was full of recliners.

"Sit here. I am going to place warm rocks on your body to relax your muscles before your massage," she said.

This is so cool, I thought as I took a seat on the wonderfully comfortable and relaxing recliner. I laid back and got comfy. Maria pulled out a towel and placed a heated stone on it. She wrapped it and then laid it on top of me. She repeated this until she had placed stones all along my body. I lay there for about fifteen minutes with my eyes closed enjoying the music playing in the background, all the while absorbing the gentle fragrance that danced through the room. I was so relaxed I was slightly startled when I felt Maria removing the stones off me while she announced it was time for my massage.

"Follow me, Mrs. Katelyn," she said as she led me into the private room that was ready for me. "Please take your robe off and slip under the sheets on the table and I will be back in a few minutes." Maria stepped away, giving me some privacy.

I did as she said and prepared to be further relaxed. Maria was scheduled for an hour-long massage and it flew by so fast it felt like ten minutes. She was either that good or I was that stressed and really needed a massage.

"All done, Mrs. Katelyn."

"What, seriously? Was that really an hour?"

Maria smiled and nodded. "Please put your robe back on and I will take you back to the recliner for some additional rock therapy."

I was given privacy again for a few minutes to put my

robe on. I had never had a massage before, never mind at a luxurious spa. Heck, the spa's bathroom may have been bigger than my entire house back in Michigan.

Maria came back, and before my hair appointment, she approached me and said, "Mrs. Katelyn, your fiancé is looking for you in the lobby of the spa. Do you need to go?"

Anxiety and uneasiness rushed through me as I began to think of possible scenarios of why he came to get me. *Is everything okay at home? Did something happen at the hotel? Did someone get hurt? Was it something at work that pissed him off?* I hurried to the locker room to get dressed, grabbed my room key and cell phone, and dashed to the front lobby of the spa. As I approached the lobby, I could see him pacing; he had a frown and was wringing his hands. I was at first worried to see him there but then was confused why he looked so angry. I couldn't figure out his reasoning for coming for me. I thanked the lady in the lobby, and Jonathan, without saying a word, stormed out of the spa. I raced behind him frantically.

"Jonathan, is everything okay? Are the girls okay? Why did you come get me?" I asked, feeling all the stress that had melted away during my spa appointment return at lightning speed and ten times stronger.

"Kate, what the hell is wrong with you? I have been trying to text you for the last three hours to see if you're okay. For all I knew you had been kidnapped and killed. This is Mexico, you know. It happens all the time."

I grabbed his hand and he jerked his arm away from me and stormed off toward our hotel room.

"Oh my goodness, what just happened? This is a five-star hotel and who has their cell phones with them during a massage?!" I yelled back at him, but he refused to listen and continued to walk to our room. I was left to follow behind with the feeling like a little girl who did something bad and was verbally disciplined by her father. I slowly made my way to our hotel room. Jonathan was on the patio having a whisky on the rocks and I curled up into a ball on the bed and began crying. *What did I do? I didn't realize I was gone for so long, but it's our wedding day and I was getting ready.* After a bit, Jonathan came over to the bed and curled up behind me. He began to stroke my hair.

"Kate, I just got so scared. I can't imagine losing you, and it's dangerous in Mexico. I could never forgive myself if something happened to you. It's why I got so mad at you. I wouldn't have gotten so furious at you if you had just answered your texts. Let's get some lunch and get ready for our big day. Today you get to wear your beautiful dress I bought for you," he said as he continued lightly stroking my hair.

I was reminded of that day I was so excited to find my dress and after that fight, I no longer really was as enthusiastic about it. I had lost a bit of the enjoyment of finding the dress of my dreams; now it was just a dress for our wedding day.

Jonathan had apologized, but my stomach was in knots. How could the happiest day of my life be starting off in tears? *I should be happy he is protective of me and wants to keep me safe, so why is my gut screaming at me? There is a lot going on today: I am away from my girls and getting married and I scared Jonathan into thinking I went missing. Naturally, my stomach is in knots*, I reasoned. *That's a lot all at once*, I thought as I cleaned up to go to lunch with Jonathan.

After lunch we headed back to our hotel room to get ready for our ceremony. We were meeting the minister at the wedding chapel at three in the afternoon and then we had a reservation for a romantic beach dinner for two at 6 p.m. We wanted to make sure we could take wedding photos and be on the beach in time to have a sunset dinner. When we got up to the room we began to get dressed and Jonathan came up behind me. He placed one hand on my breast and then another on my stomach and gently started to kiss my neck.

"Today is the day," he whispered softly in my ear. "Are you ready to be Mrs. Katelyn Price?"

He moved on to nibbling my earlobe. I giggled as he hit a ticklish spot and replied, "I sure do like the sound of that."

He slowly placed his hands on my panties and began to lower them while still kissing me.

"I want you one more time as a single woman before I make an honest woman out of you, Kate."

He stood up, bent me over, and slipped himself inside of me. Both of us enjoyed the intimacy, but he suddenly pulled out.

"I am going to leave you hanging, so you spend the entire time of our wedding day wanting more."

"Wait!" I said in anguish as I was left unsatisfied.

He smiled, turned, and headed for the bathroom to get ready. He certainly left me very wet and very horny and I could no longer think straight. The anticipation of when we were going to finish where we left off was torture. How the heck could he handle it? It was the only thing I could think about as I got dressed. Suddenly the wedding wasn't what I was thinking about; I was fantasizing about his hands all over me, and the urge to finish was overtaking my thoughts. Jonathan came out of the bathroom in his black tuxedo and he looked so amazing, it did nothing but help my desire to throw him onto the bed and make mad passionate love all night long. His tuxedo fit him so incredibly perfect that I honestly wanted him to keep it on while he fucked me that night.

"You look so handsome," I said.

I quivered with thirst for him as he walked over to me. I was in a long, silky, flowing, white spaghetti strap wedding dress with an open back and white lace flat shoes so I could stand on the beach beside Jonathan and not worry about sinking into the sand.

"You look stunning, my bride," said Jonathan as he took me in, admiring me in my gown. "Can't wait to spend the rest of my life with you."

He reached for my hand and we headed off to the wedding chapel looking fabulous. I was feeling so many emotions as we walked hand in hand and none of them were of a blushing bride. I was sad my family was not here to witness our union as husband and wife, I was highly aroused, not to mention the emotional rollercoaster I felt the night before. We arrived at the chapel where we were greeted by a wedding coordinator. She was very thorough, going over the marriage license, photo packages, and other miscellaneous items, and answering any questions we had before the ceremony. Once all the technicalities were finalized, we headed to the gazebo on the beach where the minister was waiting for us. He was a shorter, older man, with thick black hair and a black mustache. He smiled as we approached him and held out his hand to introduce himself.

"*Hola*, I am Mr. Flores. I will be performing your wedding vows. It's a pleasure to meet you both," he said as he shook Jonathan's hand first and then mine. "Are you ready to begin?"

We both nodded and he began.

"Today, you both are about to start a new chapter in your life together. Make sure you fill it with adventures, family, laughter, happiness, and love. On this day you will vow to be each other's best friend, life partner, and lover for the rest of your lives through the happy days and through the miserable, dark storms that pass over and test your marriage. Stay strong, for true love will see you through, and with communication and respect for one another, you will be stronger and grow as a couple. Will you Jonathan take Katelyn to be there through the good and bad days for as long as you both shall live?"

Jonathan looked deep into my eyes and smiled. "I do."

"Katelyn, same question?"

Not breaking from each other's stare, I replied, "I do."

The minister put his bible down, took each of our hands into his and said, "May God bless you both and your union. I now pronounce you man and wife. Jonathan, you can kiss your bride."

We kissed and the photographer who was there during the ceremony clicked away to capture the moment. Our photographer didn't speak much English so with his broken Spanish and Jonathan translating we managed to take some photos of us at various spectacular locations throughout the resort. We spent about an hour taking photos and then we headed back to the gazebo where the wedding coordinator had a cake and champagne set up on a table with a white tablecloth and rose petals scattered over the top. We toasted to each other and to our wedding day, and we each sliced a piece of wedding cake with the photographer present, ending our session with him.

As we headed along the path to the beach, we were congratulated by so many of the hotel employees and guests. It was quite sweet, but I missed not having my family and friends with us. I didn't have many friends, but my mom, girls, Scott, and my best friend would have loved to see us get married; besides, who wouldn't want to be on the beach on vacation? I would have loved to put the girls in little white flower-girl dresses and watch them happily throw rose petals. It would have been so cute. I wonder if Jonathan missed Scott. I knew teenagers could be difficult, but he would have looked so handsome in his own tux standing beside his father. We watched the sunset over the ocean while we ate surf and turf and listened to a Mexican band serenading the guests eating.

We drank wine and enjoyed the evening and then went back to the hotel room. Jonathan stopped before we entered the room, swooped me up in his arms, and walked us into our room as newlyweds.

"It's now time to make love to me. Don't take your dress off, Kate. I want you in it while I finish what I started this morning," he said as he proceeded to remove his pants and boxers and walk toward me with passion in his eyes. He placed one hand on the back of my neck, pulled me in for an incredible kiss, and then carried me to bed, lifting my dress up above my waist and making love to me.

Our trip was six days seven nights, and before I knew it, between travel days and our wedding day, we only had a couple days left to enjoy Mexico. We agreed one day we were going to relax on the beach and the other day we decided to explore downtown to buy some souvenirs. We slept in the day we decided to go shopping, made love first, and then went to eat breakfast at the resort. The shopping district was a thirty-minute walk down the beach where the resort was located. We did not blend in with the locals. With our pale skin, sunglasses, flip-flops, and camera in hand, it was clear we were tourists. The road was a pedestrians-only road, with tiny shops stacked side by side, street food vendors, and Mexican Native Indian performers dancing in the courtyards. It was a fun atmosphere. About an hour of shopping and seeing all the same trinkets in every store, Jonathan suggested we stop at a local restaurant for a drink. We headed back toward the hotel and found a quaint Mexican oyster bar overlooking the beach. We headed inside for a beer and an afternoon cocktail. We sat and enjoyed people-watching when Jonathan suggested I eat something.

"Kate, you should eat an appetizer, otherwise you will get a stomachache."

"I am not hungry right now."

"Let me order something. The smell of food will make you hungry," he persisted.

Jonathan ordered a platter of various Mexican appetizers despite my lack of interest. We sipped our drinks and chatted about my move to Chicago when we got back. The waiter showed up with our food and my husband began to display his overbearing, controlling self.

"Eat, sweetheart, you need food if you are drinking. Try it."

"No, I really don't want any. I am still full from breakfast."

"Stop being stubborn, just have some." Jonathan pushed the platter toward me.

"Jonathan, please enjoy. I am good," I repeated. I was becoming annoyed by his pushiness.

"It's particularly good and authentic. Don't be a resort snob."

"I said I am fine," I snapped and became inwardly quiet trying not to make a scene, but I was irritated at his comment and his bossiness.

Jonathan stared at me while silently eating. He called for the bill and paid with the Mexican cash he exchanged at the front desk of the resort that morning. He stood up and left me sitting at the restaurant and began walking toward the resort by himself. I didn't know whether to be livid or depressed that my husband was acting like a baby. I let him walk for about five minutes on his own and then I slowly got up from the table and began to follow him. I was nearly half a mile back behind him, and I could see he wasn't going to come back for me. He was determined on being a jackass, walking back to the resort without his wife. We were newlyweds–he was supposed to be celebrating his love, but instead he ditched me because he couldn't exert control over me. We walked separately for no reason other than I wouldn't conform to his request. I watched Jonathan head up to the resort, presumably straight to our room to pour a drink and read, while I headed toward the pool to relax and reflect. *What the hell! Is this what our marriage is going to be like? Him pouting like a child when he doesn't get what he wants? What now!* I was trying not to be pessimistic, but Jonathan was making it difficult.

I hung out at the pool until I got too hot in the sun without my swimsuit and headed to our room. I walked back feeling depressed that what should have been a fun day ended with an unnecessary argument. I opened the door and Jonathan was on the balcony with his book in one hand and beer in the other as I suspected. I went to the bathroom to shower and put on my bathing suit. When I got out Jonathan had walked in to get another beer. He took one look at me in my black bikini and came over to me.

"Where do you think you are going looking that hot without me?" With one swift hand motion he untied the strings of my tiny bikini top exposing my breasts. He leaned down and placed his mouth over my left nipple and began sucking on it while, at the same time, untying the string of my bottom bikini, letting it drop to the ground.

"You know that I can't resist you in that black bikini. Time for you to give me what I want." He turned me around so that I was facing away from him. He ran his hands all over my naked body while he whispered into my ear. "You have an amazing body, young lady." I was terribly angry at him, but those emotions were slowly dissipating. I felt like I was on an emotional roller coaster that day and I was on the thrilling part of the ride where it was time to scream with excitement. Jonathan managed to direct me toward the bed, bending me over and pinning me against it. He slowly moved his hand down my back, sending an electrifying shiver through my body. He slid his finger inside of me, and with his other hand, he unbuckled his pants. I heard his pants fall to the floor and felt him as he made his way back up kissing me softly. He stood behind me and gathered up my hair into one of his hands, using it to pull my head back. Then, without hesitation, he thrust his penis inside of me and made love to me. It was passionate, it was intense, and it was like I was making love to a completely different man.

The next day was our last at the resort before we headed back to Detroit to get me and the girls ready to move to Chicago. I was so nervous. I had so many things to think about. I had to pack all our clothes and the girls' toys and books, I had to enroll the girls into a new pre-school in Chicago, and I had to find a new job. It was all overwhelming. I couldn't let all those thoughts ruin our last day of our honeymoon, which was spent mostly in bed together making love or on the beach taking in the hot Mexican sunshine, before heading back to Michigan's cooler temperatures.

CHAPTER TEN

Compromise Goes One Way

THE NEXT MORNING, WE WERE UP AT THE CRACK of dawn waiting for our shuttle driver to take us back to the airport. We were now Mr. and Mrs. Jonathan Price, ready to begin our lives together as a blended family and I couldn't wait. I had already given my two weeks' notice before we left for our honeymoon so that when we came back, I was ready for a fresh start. It was difficult to do, and I had so many mixed emotions when I walked into my boss's office and told him. I was saddened to leave my job and my coworkers. I had made so many amazing work friendships over the years and I was good at my job. It was a bittersweet moment. I was thrilled to begin my life with Jonathan, but it was sad to say goodbye to the familiarity of my daily routine and the friendly faces of my coworkers. Change is always difficult and overwhelming, but I was focusing on the positivity of our new chapter that was about to be created. Jonathan headed back to Chicago because he had to be in the office first thing and the plan was to hire a moving company to pack up all our clothes and belongings.

Jonathan flew back to Michigan on Friday after work so he could join us on our drive to Chicago and help with our move. I had the car packed, we said goodbye to my mom with big bear hugs and kisses, and then headed off to Chicago. I was feeling homesick and we hadn't even left the driveway. Our lives were going to be so new and I was going to miss seeing my mom every day. Our first year was an adjustment. I began working in one of Chicago's steel mills as a clerk. It was an amazing change from when I worked in the steel mill in Detroit, always working overtime in a hot and dirty facility. Now I was in an office environment, and with my background and knowledge, I was able to help with the clerical work. I really enjoyed my new job, but life was still super busy.

There was so much to get accustomed to for all of us. Jonathan had to get used to having young kids in his home again with toys everywhere. Meanwhile, the girls were adjusting to being in pre-school full days when they were used to being at home with their grandmother, and I was now working all day, learning to be a wife again while still maintaining mommy duties plus adding the upkeep of a house that was four times the size I was used to. I never really had to do much of the cooking or cleaning when I lived with my mother because she took care of that for me while I worked. I didn't have anyone to help me, and Jonathan worked late hours and wasn't home early enough to assist with the day-to-day household duties. To add to the learning curve of our new life, I was also trying to connect with my fifteen-year-old stepson, but it was a bit challenging. Scott was a quiet boy who spent most of the time in his room with the door closed doing his own thing. Scott and Jonathan were not close from what I learned living with them. Scott was sadly invisible to Jonathan, and I think Scott preferred it that way. I tried to make conversation, but Scott didn't show any interest and he strangely kept his hoodie up while he roamed around the house, avoiding any possible interaction with the family. When Jonathan was with us on weekends for dinner, I noticed Scott was distant and disengaged with us. He would eat with his head face down and would devour his meal so he could be excused. Avoiding interaction with anyone was his norm. As time passed, and my relationship slightly grew with Scott, I noticed he would be more relaxed at the dinner table when Jonathan wasn't present. The girls would usually spend the entire time at dinner chitchatting and trying to engage Scott with a million questions. Scott was always polite, and occasionally I would catch a smirk when the girls were acting silly at the table. But overall, most of the time, Scott had no interest in being social.

One weekend, as we were having our morning coffee on the couch, Jonathan noticed I was unusually quiet. "I know you have had a lot of change in a short period of time. Why don't you call the local salon this morning, see if they can squeeze you in? I can take care of the girls since I have to help Scott work on his school project anyway."

I had been so busy adjusting to everything, I hadn't had time to color my hair and I had been wanting to put in some pretty highlights.

"That would be amazing, hun. Thank you, I appreciate it," I replied as I contacted the salon.

The salon near the house happened to have a cancellation that morning so I headed off to get my hair colored. When I got there, I was so excited I had them do some fun red highlights and shorten my hair to shoulder length. I thought it would be a delightful change to have shorter hair with some accenting highlights—I knew Jonathan would love it. I didn't have time to take care of my long hair and I thought it would be a great new look instead of always having it in a messy bun. The lady at the salon was very pleasant and helpful, giving me suggestions on the right highlights and hairstyle that would suit my face. I was at the salon for a couple hours, but Jonathan was texting me pretty regularly keeping me in the loop of what was going on at the house.

"Hope you're having fun, beautiful. Don't worry about anything over here. The girls are in their rooms playing with their toys and I am working with Scott on his electronic project. Just have fun."

"Thanks, sweetheart. See you soon. I'm almost done," I texted back.

"No rush. Take your time and enjoy."

When I was done, I drove straight home to show Jonathan my new look. I opened the door and he was sitting on the couch, so I went over to give him a kiss and show off my new style.

"So, what do you think?" I asked as I twirled around for him to see.

"You cut your hair?" Why?" he responded.

"I thought it would be fun with my new highlights."

"Fun? You look like a boy now," he said. "I like ladies with long hair. I didn't marry a boy."

"Don't be silly, it's still shoulder length," I replied, disappointed about his reaction to my new look.

"Did you miss what I said? You look like a boy. It's not attractive. Don't cut it again."

"Jonathan, this is my body, and I can cut it if I want to," I snapped, irritated at his demanding and dominating attitude.

Jonathan stood up, gave me a dirty look, and replied, "It's my body now; you are mine. I said it once and won't repeat myself. Don't cut your hair again." And he walked away to his den and left me standing there, slouched over with a blank face, crushed from his criticism and insulting demeanor. I went upstairs to see the girls. Hailey and Sofia had no clue what Jonathan said or that I was depressed by it. When they saw my new look, they both lit up with enthusiasm.

"Wow, Mommy, I like your new hair," said Sofia.

"Mommy, you look so pretty," Hailey followed.

Seeing the girls' enthusiasm brightened my mood. They always could make my heart smile.

The rest of the day, Jonathan gave me the cold shoulder and silent treatment. He had to punish me for doing something he didn't approve of and the fact that I disagreed with him. I was able to keep it together, but it was the most uncomfortable day. I didn't understand why he felt the need to insult me, and why he continually needed to punish me with the silent treatment. I was so irritated I was putting together a full defense argument in my head for when I saw him.

I can do what I want to my body. He doesn't own me, and we all have our own opinions. If I don't agree with him, he thinks it's acceptable to ignore me like I will give in or learn my lesson. How can he be so mean and insulting? I have never had any man call me a boy. I may not be a beautiful model or a trophy wife, but I certainly don't look like a boy. I know I am beautiful inside and out. I'm getting whiplash from him taking something out on me that he isn't happy about. Maybe he is upset because the girls did something that annoyed him in the few hours I was away. Either way, I don't deserve to have my self-esteem crushed and rejected the way he did and then be blatantly ignored as punishment. I ended up leaving and taking the girls shopping because I couldn't stand the silence. I never ended up using my defense argument because he avoided me the entire evening and went to bed early to ignore me further.

The fighting between Jonathan and me began to surface more and more every day. Jonathan would come home and complain that I wasn't at the door waiting for him with a kiss like I did in Michigan. Of course, he couldn't see that in Detroit, we would have my mother around to help with the kids. He could take me away for drinks and dinners and have me all to himself. Now it was daily homework, dinner prep, doctor appointments, and other things that he never saw when we were dating. Jonathan would get irritated when he got home and there were backpacks in the entryway, toys on the couch, and especially when there were crayons on the kitchen table. The fights progressively continued, and I couldn't do anything that wouldn't anger him. Jonathan would say I didn't care about his things in "his house."

One evening, he came home and the first thing that came out of his mouth when he saw me was, "You and the girls have no respect for other people's things. This is my house; I expect them to show some respect."

What the heck happened to "hello" or "hey sweetie"? Instead I got an insult and him now referencing "his house" as if we were just visiting. I had the bulk of the domestic responsibilities and he had the nerve to come home and take out his bad day on me. He had successfully changed my mood from happy to upset the instant he walked in the door. I placed my hand on my hip ready for a fight and snapped back.

"Excuse me, we do have respect, but they are just kids. Don't you remember when Scott was little?" I questioned him.

"Scott always played in his room. I never saw him

or his toys when he was little. Your girls have stuff everywhere. It's ridiculous!" he yelled.

"It's not normal to not see your children. We live in a time now when kids are seen and heard, you know."

"Not if I have anything to say about it."

"Well you don't thankfully; they are not your kids," I yelled back, losing control of my emotions and being hurtful with my words.

I know that he bought his home, but I couldn't understand how he expected us to feel at home when he continually referenced "his house" like we were still guests. The fighting didn't stop at the girls making normal kids' messes, and the next fight was focused on me not keeping their bedtime strict. Hailey, Sofia, and I had a routine that every evening we would watch a cartoon of their choice before bedtime. I wasn't overly strict on their bedtime, but I quickly learned his rigidness the first month we lived there. At 7:30 p.m. exactly, Jonathan came over and turned the television off while we were still watching.

"Jonathan, what did you do that for?" I asked. I tried to control my voice from rising, but my heart sped up and my face turned red as my mood shifted from relaxed to angry. I attempted to not get noticeably furious in front of the girls, but I couldn't help it. I clenched my jaw and could feel my muscles tense. *Who does he think he is taking it upon himself to shut us down whenever he pleases? I am the girls' mother and an adult; I don't need him to tell me when it's bedtime.*

"It's 7:30 p.m., Kate. Time for the girls' bedtime."

"Well, there was five minutes left."

"They can watch it tomorrow," he replied as he began to walk away.

"No, they can't. Who the hell watches the last five

minutes of a show the next day?" And with that I turned the television back on. I was now fuming. He had a lot of nerve.

Jonathan whipped around, gave me one of his many death stares–where he would look at me straight in the face for a couple minutes like he wanted to strangle me–then slammed the master bedroom door shut. The girls both looked at me, and I could see in their eyes they didn't know what to do next.

"Should we close the TV now, Mommy?" asked Sofia.

"No, baby, it's fine. Let's finish. We need to see the ending, right?" I replied, smiling at her to reassure her everything was okay, even though deep down it wasn't.

"You guys argue a lot, Mommy," Hailey whispered up to me with her hand near her mouth, as though it were a secret.

"Husbands and wives sometimes argue, sweetie. It doesn't mean we don't love each other or you two. It just means we have different opinions and that's okay," I replied.

I was trying to create an illusion that everything was okay for their sake, but if a little girl could see we argued a lot, it wasn't okay. We were clearly fighting more than normal. I didn't want them to think constant fighting was acceptable behavior. Her comment lingered in my head the rest of the evening. We finished our show and then Sofia asked me for a snack.

"Mommy, I'm hungry. Can I have something to eat?"

"Of course, sweetheart. Come with me to the kitchen. Let's get you a snack," I replied.

I made some cheese and crackers for her and Hailey. At 8:30 p.m. I tucked them into bed. The fighting was getting to the girls too because Hailey asked me directly, "Are we moving back to Grandma's house soon?"

"Why would you ask that?" I asked as I stroked her hair.

"I don't know. I was just wondering."

"No, cutie-pie, we aren't moving back to Grandma's house. Everything is good. I want you both to be happy. Are you happy?" I asked.

"Yes, Mommy," she replied. I gave them both a kiss good night and hung out on Sofia's bed, waiting for her to fall asleep. A million thoughts ran through my head: *This isn't good. The girls are feeling unsettled. They can see Jonathan's looks of intimidation and my mood shifts.* He didn't intimidate me; he only aggravated me with his lack of respect he had toward me as his equal. He had changed when we moved in. He went from having fun with the girls playing games and watching shows with them to being uninterested and distant. Now he didn't have time for "silly" games or to watch cartoons. We were a blended family by marriage, but most of the time I felt like our families never really blended at all and we were living separate lives.

That fight was the beginning of what I knew our new life was going to look like with Jonathan. I was becoming unhappy and regretting my choice. My life before was hard and we didn't have much, but there was laughter, and the carefree, fun times we had disappeared here in Chicago. Thoughts of regret filled my head and the notion that I had made a mistake marrying Jonathan was wearing on me.

I headed for our bedroom to start what was going to be a daily fight with Jonathan. As soon as I walked in, I could see Jonathan was reading his book, and caught a glimpse of the frustration on his face because he lost control of the evening. I was irritated that he expected me to tolerate his childish behavior, not to mention the uncomfortable tension that he created for no reason. When I walked in, he refused to look up to acknowledge me, but I was feeling resentful and didn't care; I let him have a piece of my mind, anyway.

"What is your problem? It was very rude for you to turn off the TV like that. We were all sitting there enjoying our show. It's like you can't stand seeing anyone happy," I said, accusing him of being a miserable person.

"It was their bedtime, and I don't appreciate your disrespecting our relationship like that," he replied.

"Disrespect? The only disrespect I saw today was from you. It's not acceptable for you to try to undermine me as a parent. What makes you think you have any authority to override my decision to let them finish their show?" I said, and I stormed off into the bathroom, not giving him an opportunity to reply. When I came out, Jonathan had shut off the lights and rolled over so that his back was facing me. I climbed into bed and reciprocated the cold shoulder and we didn't talk any further that night. *He owes me an apology for being rude*, I thought to myself. We went to sleep not discussing anything and once again leaving another argument open and unresolved. At four in the morning, I felt Jonathan make his way over to me. *He is going to apologize*, I thought, but instead he began to fondle me. *I guess our fight is over. Is this how we are going to "resolve" issues, with sleepy sex?* I was not sure what to think. He left me feeling robbed of an apology and powerless by not acknowledging my decision to keep the girls up a little longer before bed. We had sex but not with any intimacy because I had no closure to our argument and he clearly didn't take my position on our argument seriously enough; he satisfied himself that morning and went back to sleep peacefully. *Well, this must be a new way to make up. Not sure if that was his apology, but I am not going to dwell on it any further. Life is too short to fight over the little stuff or keep fighting.* He left his hand on my breast while he was sleeping. I couldn't get comfortable enough to sleep because my breasts were very tender, and the weight of his hand was hurting me. I gently slipped his hand off my breast and tried to find a comfortable sleeping position. Jonathan immediately placed his hand back on my breast, still seemingly asleep, and once again I slipped it off. This continued a couple more times until I turned to him and said, "Jonathan, stop it."

"No, these are mine; I will do what I want," he replied as he once again placed his hand on my breast, this time clenching it and smiling. I whipped his hand off.

"Jonathan, I said no, stop it. I can't sleep that way, it hurts," I exclaimed, getting extremely irritated he wasn't listening or respecting me.

"I don't believe I am hurting you; I will sleep how I want to, and I will squeeze your breasts when I want to. And I want to sleep while holding your breast," he said. I slapped his hand away.

"This is my body, not yours, and I said stop it!" At this point it was almost time for me to get up, so I got dressed and left the room, slamming the door behind me while trembling with rage. I headed to the kitchen to make coffee, but my hands were shaking from my nerves having to defend myself against my husband.

My mind was spinning now.

What is wrong with him? Does he think he is entitled to my body? I can't believe he is trying to exert sexual domination over me. How can my husband be so degrading and not care at all about me? Why would I lie and say I was in pain, or does he not have any empathy for me at all? We are supposed to be in love–we are newlyweds still, but I don't feel loved. I regret even marrying him. It can't be normal for a man to be that inconsiderate, waking his wife up to pleasure himself without any regard to my sleep or my own pleasures, and then going back to sleep. I can't keep fighting, but this is no longer the little stuff; this is clearly a disregard toward my feelings and my body.

When Jonathan finally woke up and got ready for work, he came out and tried to kiss my forehead. I backed away and his eyes widened.

"What do you think you are doing, young lady? Come give me a kiss goodbye."

My eyes glassed up. "No, I will not. You owe me an apology," I replied.

"An apology for what? You're my wife. I have nothing to apologize for. Now come here and give me a kiss," he said as he grabbed my arm and pulled me in. "Stop being feisty and overdramatic, it's not a good look for you. I will see you tonight." He slapped my ass and walked away, not concerned or interested in talking about why I was so upset. The lack of communication in fights was deteriorating our relationship. Somehow, he was able to make me feel like I was being fussy and dramatic while he went about his day, leaving me anxious and distressed.

That evening, after the girls went to bed, we began our nightly routine of him climbing into bed to read a book while I showered. Usually our routine did not consist of absolutely any conversation or discussions about our day. Instead, the end of the evening looked more like me getting into bed, Jonathan sliding under the comforter to pleasure me, and then climbing on top to fuck me. Tonight I decided I was going to change up the routine and I stopped him when he closed his book and got ready to go under the covers to kiss me.

"Hun, can't we talk first before we go straight to having sex?" I asked.

"No, hun, we tried that once before and you ended up falling asleep after we chatted and then I didn't get to end the night being with you."

"Okay, if I fall asleep, you can make it up with sleepy sex," I replied.

But that was a mistake on my part because we chatted that night and the next morning I woke up with a headache and couldn't fulfill my promise for sleepy sex. Jonathan was so irate. He got up from bed and began banging doors in the bathroom and closet as he got dressed. Then I heard a door slam. He had left for work and had reacted negatively that he didn't get laid. Throughout the day we text fought. Jonathan began blowing up my phone with his disappointment.

"I don't appreciate you lying to me, Kate. You said if we chatted like you wanted, we would play the next morning. How dare you wake up and blow me off with such a pitiful excuse?" was the first text I received the moment he got to work.

"Jonathan, I didn't lie. I woke up with a pounding headache. I don't appreciate you being so selfish. One night isn't a big deal."

"Are you saying having sex with me isn't a big deal? You need to rethink your word choices, Kate."

"I wasn't saying that. I said if we can't be intimate one night on account of one of us not feeling well it's no big deal."

"Just because you have a headache doesn't mean I should suffer," he replied.

The texting continued. Jonathan wasn't being

reasonable and my having a headache that morning was an excuse and not an acceptable one. He continued fighting with me the whole day via text. We couldn't communicate at night because sex was a priority so other than the text exchanges throughout the day, we seriously lacked any communication, and any concerns I needed to discuss became a text fight, which happened more often than not.

When Jonathan got home, he decided to briefly talk after I got out of the shower. His topic of choice was to tell me why he was so strict about bedtime.

"Kate, do you know why I am so annoyed about you missing bedtime with the girls?" he asked out of the blue as I got into bed.

I didn't say it out loud but thought, *because you're a control freak?*

I shrugged my shoulders. "No, why," I replied.

"It's because I just want to spend as much time with you as I can. We don't get a lot of time together because of my crazy work schedule. Is compromising a possibility? Maybe you can start their show earlier so that you can make their bedtime? You realize it's not the five minutes; it's the snacks after and then bathroom breaks. Before you know it, the girls are extending their bedtime 30 minutes, then an hour–it just keeps getting longer."

I was ashamed of myself and guilty of thinking the worst in Jonathan. He just wanted to spend time with me, but he didn't approach the subject well. I took offense and started a fight with him. How could I be so selfish? I should've known he was stressed from his long days at work, and instead of compromising, I overreacted. This fight was my fault. Jonathan had a point, so I agreed to his request of starting the girls' evening routine earlier so that they were in bed at their normal bedtime.

Unfortunately, the desire of needing to control all things in his surroundings became more evident in various situations. I realized this one day when I told him I needed to see a doctor for a bladder infection.

"Make sure you see a female doctor," Jonathan demanded before I went to make my appointment.

"I will ask but I don't care who it is so long as they can prescribe medication," I snapped back, feeling the discomfort of my bladder contracting like it was a heart pumping blood throughout my body.

"Which part of *you will only see a female doctor* don't you understand? I will not accept you going to a male doctor," he replied.

"What are you talking about, Jonathan? I had a male doctor in Michigan; he was the one that delivered the girls."

"We weren't married then; no other man will see my wife naked except for me."

I wasn't going to fight about something as small as who I saw so I gave in and found a female doctor.

"Jonathan, can you stay with the girls so I can go?"

"We are all going with you," he said.

Does he not trust I found a female doctor? I thought.

We all drove to the walk-in clinic and Jonathan stayed in the waiting room with Hailey and Sofia when it was my turn to go in. While I patiently waited for the doctor to come in, I noticed my phone was blowing up with texts from Jonathan.

"What's going on? Don't take your clothes off. Make sure she has a nurse with her."

I didn't know which part to address first.

"I'm still waiting," I replied.

The doctor knocked on the door, walked in when she heard me acknowledge her, sat down on the doctor stool chair in the room, and introduced herself.

"Hello, my name is Doctor Howard. What can I help you with?" she asked.

"Hello, doctor, I believe I have a bladder infection."

"What are your symptoms?" she asked.

"It stings a lot when I go to the bathroom."

"Okay, take this sample bottle and fill it up to the black line, and then come back and we will test your urine," she said.

I headed to the bathroom and replied to Jonathan who had been texting me nonstop about what was going on.

"I'm fine. I am just going to pee in a cup."

"Don't take off your clothes."

I got the antibiotics I needed for my infection, and we all headed home. That evening I could not make love because of my painful bladder. Jonathan didn't pressure me to make love knowing I was in discomfort, but he still requested I pleasure him with my mouth instead. He didn't seem to have any empathy toward my health issue and felt it was my duty as his wife. I didn't want to argue or stress myself out with his constant punishing tactics, so I gave in. I was tired and my bladder was killing me with a nonstop pulsing sensation and a strong persistent urge to urinate that made it so uncomfortable, but I kissed and sucked like the best of them to make sure he would leave me alone. He passed out immediately after he finished, and I stayed up wide awake thinking. The doctor's office revealed Jonathan's true colors. It was an eye-opening moment, and I realized how much of a controlling person Jonathan was who lacked compassion for me. He was not the man I thought I loved. How did he manage to mask it all those months we were dating, or did I miss the signs and the red flags?

CHAPTER ELEVEN

Expecting The Unexpected

OUR FIRST YEAR TOGETHER AS A MARRIED COUPLE was not at all what I was expecting. I knew we had to compromise and learn what being together every day felt like, but I never expected the constant bickering. I guess every married couple goes through an adjustment phase, but things didn't get better as time went by. Our second and third years were an uphill battle. We fought almost daily about silly things, not to mention Jonathan's entitlement he had over me that I found troubling, causing me to emotionally pull away.

I was homesick, and I was having a difficult time meeting friends here in Chicago. I was finding that other than my mom on the phone, I really had no one to confide in. Jonathan never had time and when he did, I had to be choosey on my topic of choice to avoid another argument. I told Jonathan how I was feeling one night and how I didn't have any friends.

"You realize it's your fault you don't have friends. You haven't tried; you are being antisocial. Try making an effort to get to know the ladies in the neighborhood," he suggested.

I knew I hadn't been very social in Michigan, but I didn't feel it was because I didn't want to. I was always very social in high school, going to parties and having fun. Being a young mom of two girls and working crazy hours was what changed my partying habits. It wasn't my fault I didn't have friends here either. I was new to Chicago and was still learning the ropes. I longed to be social and have a friend here in Chicago, especially since I didn't even have my mom close by. It was just me here in this big city, and it made me feel powerless and isolated.

I decided Jonathan was right, so when I saw on Facebook that the neighborhood page had a ladies' night, I asked him to watch the girls so I could go out.

"What? Absolutely not. You don't even have time for a date night, and you want to go out for ladies' night? Why don't you put this much effort into our relationship? We need to have more date nights; once every two weeks isn't enough."

I was so confused and flustered. He managed to twist everything he said. First, he suggested I go out to meet friends, and the moment I decide to do it, he yelled and said I didn't spend enough time on our relationship. *I can never do anything right.* Jonathan came to see where I was and noticed I was down.

"It's not that I won't watch the girls, hun, but I just want you to focus that energy on us."

"Jonathan, I haven't been out yet with anyone."

"Don't worry, Kate, we will make it happen. Just not this weekend, is that okay?"

I nodded with acceptance. I surrendered because I was worn out from all the fighting. I would hear him suggest one thing and then fight about it later, saying I was crazy or had heard it wrong. I couldn't seem to do anything right, and every time I opened my mouth to say something, an argument would break out. It was clear to me the same patterns that Jonathan exhibited were not going to change. The constant fighting and degrading statements he would make either during our conversation or during our fighting were getting me down.

My niece's wedding was the following weekend in New York, and I asked my mom to spend the week with us so she could join us on our road trip. We planned to be out of the house Friday before sunrise. We had decided on driving straight through to get to the hotel that evening for the wedding on Saturday afternoon. Then we intended to head out first thing Sunday morning and make it back home. The wedding wasn't until six in the evening so I made plans to take the girls to the Statue of Liberty so they could witness the famous national monument. Jonathan drove early in the morning and we all dozed off in the car. I woke up about an hour into our drive to notice the GPS was turned off.

"Jonathan, why is the GPS off? Why are we headed back to the house?" I asked.

"Don't worry about it, Kate," he replied, brushing me off like it was none of my business.

"Don't tell me not to worry about it. We are wasting time. Why are we returning?"

"I brought my pistol but have since decided to leave it at home."

My face turned red. How can a smart man think it's acceptable to bring a firearm to New York City–one of the highest touristic locations? What was he thinking? I didn't want to start a fight in the car with the girls and my mom all asleep, but I was red in the face and I was clenching my teeth to keep from pulling my hair and freaking out in the car. *Is he trying to sabotage the trip*, I thought. I was beside myself with anger.

When we finally got to New York, it was extremely late, and when we got to the front desk, they didn't have my mom's room reserved. After some arguing with the manager and finding out that the entire hotel was booked due to weddings and conferences, I told my mom she could stay with us on the pullout couch.

"Excuse me, Kate, but you need to find another room for your mother. I am a grown-ass man; I refuse to sleep with your mother."

"Don't worry, you aren't sleeping with my mother, Jonathan; she will be on the couch."

"Absolutely not, find her another room now."

"Listen, it's late, everyone is exhausted, and we are not going to waste time looking for another hotel or room. If you want to, be my guest. In the meantime, I am going upstairs with my mother and the girls to get a good night's rest." I took my key card and we left him in the lobby standing by himself, frowning and bright red in the face. I got up to the room and placed the girls in one of the queen beds and my mom went to bed on the pullout couch. I went to bed but couldn't sleep knowing Jonathan was going to make it miserable for me in some way. He finally did crawl into bed. I pretended I was asleep so I wouldn't have to deal with him. Jonathan decided he wasn't going to let anyone stop him and he began to try to put his hand down my PJ pants. I snatched his hand out immediately.

"What the hell are you doing? My mom and the kids are in the room."

"That was your choice to have your mom and the kids here with us," he said, trying to get back in my pants.

“Stop it,” I whispered with an almost quiet scream and sat up. I was trying to remain quiet to not wake anyone, but Jonathan wasn’t making it easy.

“What’s your problem?” Jonathan whispered.

“Are you kidding me right now? Go to sleep. We have a long day tomorrow. If you can’t, go somewhere else. I don’t care,” I demanded in the quietest way possible. Jonathan stood up and left the room, not to be seen until about four in the morning. I heard him come back in, and I pretended to be asleep. I had no idea where he spent most of the night. I could only imagine it was at the bar. When everyone woke up, we got ready and headed out to see the Statue of Liberty. Jonathan claimed he needed to make some work calls and disappeared, leaving my mom, me, and the girls to go sightseeing by ourselves. We took a taxi to the Statue, went on the ferry ride that took us in a loop around it, and then we took a cab back to the hotel. I texted Jonathan on our way back to let him know what we were doing.

“Hey hun, we are going to grab a quick bite before the wedding. Want to join us?”

“I will see you when you get back. I have to make some more work calls.” We headed off to get some pizza in the hotel restaurant. Jonathan was in the room when we got back, already dressed in his suit and ready to go to the wedding. We had a wonderful evening dancing. Jonathan sat at the table with my mother most of the night watching the girls and me dance together on the dance floor. He managed to dance with me a couple times during the slow dances, but there was radio silence between us and an uncomfortable awkwardness like I was dancing with a stranger. It was time for us to get the girls to bed, and we all said goodbye to the happy couple and my aunt who was smiling from ear to ear that her daughter was married.

“It was a beautiful wedding. Congratulations,” Jonathan said to my aunt Barbra.

“Thank you for coming. I am so happy you could make the drive,” replied my aunt. “If you all want, we have paid for breakfast for the family at the hotel you’re staying at. Will you join us before you head back?” she asked.

“We would love that,” I replied, giving my aunt a big hug. “Love you. Congratulations. So happy we could be here. We are going to put the girls to bed and will see you all in the morning.”

At five the next morning, Jonathan woke me up. “Let’s go, we have a long drive ahead of us.”

“What are you talking about? We told my aunt we are having breakfast with them this morning.”

“You told your aunt, I didn’t. I don’t appreciate you holding me hostage here. I never agreed to staying for breakfast. I have a right mind to leave you, your mother, and the girls here and go home.”

“Go ahead, Jonathan, leave. I will rent a car and find my own way home,” I whispered back.

“No, you know what, I will stay. I don’t want your family to think I am an asshole,” he replied. “And when we get home, you can find somewhere else to sleep. I am going to divorce your selfish, no-good-for-a-wife ass,” he said in a harsh whisper and turned his body over to give me the cold shoulder again. I was finished with this marriage. I wasn’t sure what my next step was, but I was fed up with his constant abuse.

I was devastated, confused, hurt, and angry all at once. After three years of marriage and I was already getting divorced and moving the girls back to Michigan with my mother. How did that happen?

The morning came quick and we all got packed. My mind was so emotionally drained, I couldn't think. Jonathan, on the other hand, was very cheerful putting on a wonderful show for my mother, the girls, and my family at breakfast. We stayed for a few hours visiting with my mom's family and the newlyweds, and then started our long trek home. We got home considerably late that evening, and Jonathan and I carried the sleepy girls in from the car to their bedroom. My mom took the guest room, and when everyone disappeared into their rooms, I went to sleep on the couch and sobbed into the throw pillow I was using to rest my head. Around two in the morning I felt Jonathan over me trying to wake me up.

"Come on, my love, come to bed. You know you can't live without me."

"What are you doing?" I asked, confused about his actions.

"Come, sweetness, come to our bed where you belong."

I stood up and went to bed with him. He let me get in and fall asleep, and within a couple hours, he was up wanting to have sex. Once again, he had his way with me and rolled over, content. I was baffled and laid there in silence. I took a deep breath in and slowly let it out, trying to capture my thoughts. *Is he not divorcing me now? What was he so mad about in the first place? Are we putting this fight on the back burner like nothing happened–just like the other fights?* I rolled over and quietly wept.

We were going through a rough patch. I was sure with some effort on my part we could make it work. I needed to figure out how to end all the fighting; it was not good for my stress level and it was not good for the girls. I was starting to notice I was changing; I was becoming less spontaneous and carefree. I was now more reluctant to watch one more cartoon with the girls just because it was a weekend or play in the living room with their toys. I wanted to avoid fighting with Jonathan about the house being a mess. I was changing and I didn't like it. Before I met Jonathan, I was healthy, energetic, fun, friendly, and full of life. Now I was no longer that person. I was always stressed, anxious, nervous, unhappy, angry–even overweight. I knew I needed to change something, but I didn't want to be divorced for a second time and be thought of as a loser. We tried to go on a date night to see if that would help bring back what we had–that chemistry, that passion. I had arranged for a babysitter since it was during the week. Jonathan and I had made a reservation for 6:30 p.m. and he got home from work to pick me up. The babysitter was a teenager from the neighborhood, and she had texted me she was running late. Jonathan began to pace and became irritated with me.

"Why didn't you plan this better? I can't believe I left work early for this."

"It's not my fault the babysitter is running late. It's not like we can leave before she arrives," I yelled back and now I was not in the mood to go out. I had made the arrangements, and to be fair to the young lady who was watching the girls, I kept our date, but I was so irritated I became quiet. I was tired of his passive-aggressive nature and ability to spoil the fun moments. The sitter arrived and we pulled out for dinner. I remained somber the entire drive to the restaurant.

"What's wrong with you? It's clear you don't want to be out with me on this date."

"I'm fine, just looking out the window," I answered back without giving him eye contact.

"You know what, I am not hungry." And Jonathan spun

the car around and returned to the house.

I was so embarrassed, I felt the need to lie to the sweet babysitter who already was stressed out for being late, and told her Jonathan received an urgent work request and we had to come back. I paid her in full and thanked her for her time. Jonathan and I were clearly struggling, and it wasn't getting any better.

During our fourth Christmas together as a married couple, we were invited for Jonathan's work Christmas party, which was our first year going. Normally Jonathan didn't want to attend, but this year was more of a formal event meant only for the upper managers. It was a black-tie event, with dinner, drinks, and dancing. After dinner when the band started to play, I excused myself from the table to go to the bathroom.

"Jonathan, I am going to the bathroom. Do you want me to get you another beer on my way back?" I asked.

"Yes, please," he replied politely as he smiled to the surrounding coworkers and their wives that we were sitting with for dinner.

On my way back I stopped at the bar.

"What will you have, miss?" asked the very well-dressed, handsome bartender with a British accent.

"Vodka and orange juice, and a beer," I replied.

"Sorry, madam, but we ran out of orange juice. Do you have another choice?" he asked.

"Oh okay, glass of your sweetest white house wine, I guess."

The lady beside me leaned over and said, "What bar runs out of orange juice? It's my go-to drink too. I was also denied," she said.

I laughed. "My name is Katelyn." I held out my hand for a handshake.

"I'm Lucy, nice to meet you!"

"Does your husband work at the company?" I asked.

"Yes, it's his first year. We have no idea who anyone is!"

"I'm in the same boat! I know nobody!" I replied enthusiastically. I was happy I had met someone at the party I could chat with other than my husband.

"Well then, we will be the bar sisters!" she joked.

We chuckled and chatted and were having so much fun. We carried on like a couple high-school teenagers at the bar. It was refreshing to laugh again.

We swapped numbers, and when I looked at my phone to program Lucy's number in, I realized I had been at the bar for 45 minutes and had 15 messages.

"Wow, you're a popular lady," she said, noticing my phone.

When I opened the messages icon, I realized it was Jonathan who had blown up my phone. "Oops, I better get going. I forgot I was supposed to bring my husband his beer! Let's have coffee soon!" I suggested, giving her a hug goodbye.

"Sounds good! Have a good evening," said Lucy.

I wandered back to the table Jonathan and I were assigned to, but Jonathan wasn't there. I waited at the table thinking he was probably in the bathroom. While I waited, I read his messages.

"Well, Kate, if you think you can have so much fun without me, you can figure out how to get home without me too!"

"How dare you leave me all alone at my work party all night long! I was left looking like an idiot to the people at the table we were at because my wife was at the bar the whole night. I am waiting for an apology here in my car. I almost left you completely but instead I got gas and am waiting at the gas station. Apologize and I will come pick you up, otherwise you can call an Uber. You're a selfish, selfish, inconsiderate woman."

I couldn't believe it. *How dare he leave me at this party by myself! How dare he give me an ultimatum!* I should have been shocked by his behavior, but surprisingly I wasn't. *What makes him think I will apologize for meeting another guest and having fun? It's not like I was flirting with another man. I won't apologize for being social, and if I have to, I will find my own way home.*

I stayed another hour so that Jonathan could go home, but it was the worst hour of my life. I sat there wondering how I could be treated so badly by the person who had vowed to love and cherish me. *Why does he want to isolate me from others? And how could he risk my safety and leave me stranded like this?* I called an Uber and made my way home to a locked bedroom door. I lay down on the coach and went to sleep sobbing at how my life had turned out. I was better off alone and struggling to pay the bills than living as a kept woman who was unhappy and mistreated.

The next two days I received the silent treatment from Jonathan. He woke up at 4:30 in the morning, left the house by 5 a.m. before my alarm went off, and didn't come home until 9:30 in the evening when I was already asleep in bed. I didn't hear one word from him or receive one text. On the second night, the girls and I were having dinner together.

"Mommy, why doesn't Jonathan have dinner with us anymore?" asked Hailey.

"He has been busy at work a lot."

"He isn't mad at us, is he?" asked Sofia.

"Of course not, why would you say that?" I asked, my eyes wide open that they not only noticed the distance that Jonathan and I had but that they were blaming themselves.

"Because he doesn't play with us anymore like he used to," replied Sofia.

"Sweetheart, no, never think we are mad at either of you. You are both amazing and wonderful and we love you very much. You could never do anything to make us angry at you. Okay, sweetheart?" I replied with anguish in my voice. On the third evening of silence after I had wronged him at the party, Jonathan broke the silence when he climbed into bed, cuddled behind me, and woke me up with his penis inside of me finishing. The fourth day I began receiving texts like nothing had happened between us. It was like he was bipolar, and I felt like I was living with Dr. Jekyll and Mr. Hyde. It was confusing and stressful and left me with a whirlwind of emotions. My mind was in chaos–I didn't know what to think, and my stomach was all tied up in knots. Jonathan seemed to thrive on making me anxious, clouded, and mentally exhausted all the time. I had made good friends with Lucy during all of this and began to confide in her what was going on and how Jonathan was acting. We met in secret so that Jonathan didn't know because he would get jealous that I was paying attention and making time for someone other than him.

The next year, our fifth year of marriage, things only got worse. The fighting was the same but now I was getting nonstop sarcastic stabs about how dirty the house was, how I didn't dress as nice anymore, and how I needed to work on my bedroom skills. I was starting to feel more anxious, and I noticed that the few days Jonathan came home before me, I would let out a sigh of exasperation when I would see his car in the driveway. This wasn't the happily ever after I was dreaming of. I began having regular coffee and lunch dates with Lucy, and she became my confidant and the person I relied on.

"Kate, you need to start planning to leave Jonathan before he gives you an anxiety attack. Girl, you're a basket case. He's toxic."

"I know, Lucy. I just don't know how to leave him yet. I still haven't got the strength. Thank you so much for being my friend and listening to me. I don't know how I would have survived without you. So thankful we met at that party that night."

"I am here for you, girl. I just wish you would leave that jerk. He is making your life hell," replied Lucy. I could see she was concerned for me. "Kate, I think he's a narcissist. You can never win with a narcissist."

I didn't know what that was. I went home that night and googled everything I could read about what a narcissist was. The more I read, the more I realized Lucy was right. I had married a narcissist. Jonathan checked off every narcissistic characteristic there was, and our relationship went through every textbook phase narcissists use to manipulate and control their victims. The love-bombing, isolation, and devaluing phases. I unknowingly slipped into every one of the phases and now I needed to figure out how to move on. The Christmas party where Jonathan felt he could abandon me was the best thing that had happened to me. Unexpectedly meeting Lucy utterly save me and kept me positive and sane. I couldn't walk away just yet; I had my girls I needed to think about and their stability. I decided I was going to try to make it better. He was my husband and, for better or worse, I needed to put in my best effort to save our marriage.

One day we all decided to go out for a pizza dinner with Scott and the girls. Jonathan was at work, so the plan was to meet him at the restaurant, which was on his way home. Traffic was insane in Chicago with all the road construction. It was faster for us to meet him there as opposed to waiting for him to pick us up and then fight through rush-hour traffic. When we got to the restaurant, I made sure to get a booth for Jonathan. We ordered drinks and I had a beer waiting for him when he pulled in. We ordered a large pepperoni pizza for the kids, and Jonathan and I ordered a salad each. While we were waiting for our food, I approached Jonathan about going to see my mom for the weekend with the girls. I hadn't visited her the entire time we were in Chicago, and I missed her very much. Jonathan became displeased and began to get defensive like I was provoking an argument.

"Why are you looking to start a fight?" he asked.

"I'm not, I'm just telling you what I want to do with the girls this weekend. Why is that looking for a fight?"

"Invite her here. I don't approve of you going with the girls for the weekend and leaving me here. What kind of wife goes away to her parents without her husband?"

What does he mean by "approve"? I don't need permission from anyone, and I am a damn good wife. I am not leaving him to go to sleep with another man! I didn't want to make a big scene at the restaurant, so without fighting about his very possessive, jealous, and controlling comments toward me, I replied with a lighter response to keep the conversation from getting out of hand in front of the kids and in public.

"Stop being so jealous that I am not spending every waking moment with you. It's just a weekend trip to visit with my mom; it's not a big deal and I haven't seen her in almost five years. I would invite you, but we are going to do some fun girl stuff. It is a girls' weekend," I replied.

Jonathan stood up, threw forty dollars on the table, turned to Scott, and said, "We're leaving," before walking off and leaving us there at the restaurant like scum. I was beginning to resent him more every day. These were not day-to-day marital fights. How could my husband just walk off and leave his wife and stepchildren at a restaurant and throw forty dollars on the table like I was some hooker? I felt so embarrassed and awkward. What must the surrounding people be thinking? And worse, what did the girls think when he got up and left? I told them he needed to rush back to work, but deep down, I was hurt and humiliated. He left me feeling insignificant and unworthy of his presence because of something I wanted, that he didn't approve of. I went home, packed up the girls, and we left for the weekend. Jonathan wasn't home when we got back from the restaurant. I was suspicious of where he was, but I wasn't going to stick around to keep arguing about visiting my mother, so the girls and I left. Jonathan disappeared a lot, and I hated it. For all I knew he had another woman, but I never hired a private detective to validate where he would go when he disappeared. He always deflected my questions of where he was with a comment of how it was my fault. He would say things like, "If you wouldn't make me mad, I wouldn't have to leave," and "You should trust me, I am your husband." And then he would change the conversation to how I could have made the situation better so that it wouldn't have escalated to him needing space.

That night, we got to Michigan late and I stayed up with my mom all night talking. I missed her so much and I needed to tell her what I was experiencing in my marriage. How things had changed and how he had become such a different man. I needed advice on what I should do now that my marriage was over, and I was done trying so hard to mend it.

"Mom, I don't understand his mood swings. He becomes mad so quickly and about such strange things but will role-play like he's totally fine in front of others. I have never known anyone that can mask himself as well as he can. We could be in a huge fight, and if a neighbor stops by, he changes. He becomes polite, charming, and gives off an impression that we are in love. He goes as far as putting his hand on my back and fake smiling and calling me pet names. Meanwhile, he and I are at each other's throats."

"I can't believe you haven't told me any of this before, Kate. Why? I am your mother; you know I am always here for you."

"I didn't want you to hate him, and I didn't really understand what was going on. I was trying to make it work, Mom. I don't want to be divorced again," I replied, saddened by the thought of another failed marriage.

"Do you think Jonathan is bipolar?"

"I did at first until my girlfriend mentioned narcissism. I did a lot of reading and I think she is right. I am not sure I can continue with this man. He is always arguing, insulting, calling me crazy–I can't keep this up. I am afraid I am going to have an anxiety attack."

I was so happy that night. It was a relief to talk to someone other than Lucy about what I was experiencing. Jonathan never had any idea that Lucy knew everything that was going on in our marriage. She was my best friend in Chicago, the one I called. Sometimes, when Jonathan wouldn't go somewhere with me and the girls, Lucy would join me with her daughter Chloe, and we would spend the day at the zoo or park without Jonathan ever knowing who I was with. Lucy was my savior in Chicago, but it's true when they say there is no place like being home with your mama.

That weekend in Michigan was so much fun and so needed. My mom, Hailey, Sofia, and I shopped for clothes, went to a movie, and stayed up watching cartoons and eating popcorn. There was no one to tell me what to do, no one to wake me up in the middle of the night for sleepy sex, and no text arguments. As a matter of fact, my phone was silent the whole weekend, which was not normal for Jonathan. I had a completely uninterrupted visit, which was Jonathan's way of punishing me. He was trying to torment me with the silent treatment. Ironically, it backfired because I was relieved to have no contact with him.

Sunday night I got home to find an empty house. Scott was with his mom, where he spent most of his time, and Jonathan was nowhere to be seen. I got the girls ready for bed and headed to bed myself. I was in our bedroom, walking toward our bathroom, when I noticed Jonathan's wedding band on his nightstand.

I immediately picked up the phone to call my mother.

"Mom, what does it mean when Jonathan takes his wedding band off and leaves it on his nightstand? Do you think he is with another woman?"

"Check Find My Phone; see where he is."

Jonathan had shut off his location, so it was clear he didn't want me to know where he was.

"I am going to bed, Mom. Call you tomorrow," I said, and I climbed into bed with tears in my eyes, thinking about how my marriage was over. Jonathan was cheating on me and I honestly didn't know if I cared. *Was this marriage all a waste? Is this how it ends–with Jonathan cheating? Do I hire a private detective to make sure, or does it even matter because I no longer care enough to try? This marriage has been all but happy. It has been exhausting and challenging and now it ends with betrayal. I left my life in Michigan for nothing.* I took a photo of his wedding band and sent it to Jonathan with a caption "Did you forget something?" and then went to bed.

The next morning, I was getting the girls ready for school and something felt wrong.

I still hadn't heard from Jonathan from the weekend or in response to my photo text I sent him. How could he treat me like this? How could someone be so cold and cruel? We were supposed to spend the rest of our lives together and he was possibly out making a fool of me with another woman. That night he still didn't come home and the next morning I woke up in an empty bed. My bed wasn't the only thing empty; I felt depressed, lost, and alone inside. I went about my morning to get the girls ready, but I felt chest pain, had a dry mouth, was having difficulty swallowing and breathing, and suddenly had a rapid heartbeat. *Am I having a heart attack?* I thought.

I stopped what I was doing and sat down to take some deep breaths, but I didn't feel any relief. I had no idea what was happening to my body right then. I knew I had to get the girls ready and drop them off quickly so that I could go immediately to urgent care. I continued about our morning routine so that the girls didn't know what was happening, but it was everything I could do to continue without feeling like I was going to faint.

We got into the car and I drove them to their elementary school, giving a kiss and hug to Hailey and Sofia when I dropped them off. I thought that if this was a heart attack, I didn't know whether I would see the girls again. I got into my car, texted Jonathan that I was headed to urgent care because I thought I was having a heart attack, and then drove off crying hysterically all the way to urgent care. I received a text from Jonathan that he had left work and was on his way to meet me. I got to urgent care first, checked in at the front desk, and told them my symptoms. They immediately brought me in based on my symptoms of a patient experiencing cardiac arrest. When Jonathan arrived, I was already in a hospital robe and hooked up to multiple medical devices.

Jonathan took notice of me in the hospital bed and said, "You took your clothes off? Isn't this a bit overdramatic?"

"This is what they do when they are checking for a heart attack," I replied sarcastically. I was irritated by his comments and lack of empathy toward me, so I looked away and rolled my eyes. Had he just come to the hospital to criticize me? He sat down in the chair beside my bed.

"Why don't you sound happy I'm here?" he questioned me. He still hadn't said hello or asked how I was feeling at that point. "Don't you want me here, or do you want me to go?" he snapped.

"Do whatever you need to do, Jonathan. I am worried and am not going to look happy," I replied, not giving a damn whether he stayed with me or left.

The nurse came in and said, "Can you walk? We need to do an x-ray."

I nodded. She came over and helped me get up, and with one hand on the back of my robe and the other holding the IV that was on a hanger with wheels, I went with her to get an x-ray. It was a quick chest x-ray, and when I came back and got back into the urgent care bed, Jonathan again was insensitive to my situation and asked, “Did you keep your robe on?”

I rolled my eyes and before I could answer the nurse came back in to tell me the doctor was on their way in. After about twenty-five minutes of waiting for the doctor, he finally came in to tell us my test results.

“Hello, my name is Doctor Abbott. I see you have had some concerning symptoms.”

“Yes, doctor, is it something serious?” I replied with worry in my tone.

“Looking at the test results, everything came back fine.”

“But, doctor, why did I have those symptoms? It really felt like a heart attack,” I replied, concerned about what I felt and wanting answers.

“Honestly, I am not sure,” he said. “Did you do anything strenuous, or are you possibly under some high stress? Those are sometimes two reasons that we see heart attack symptoms that don’t show up as anything we need to treat.”

“Not that I know of. I appreciate your time. Thanks, doctor,” I replied.

I slowly gathered my purse and coat. I wished I had gotten a better answer other than I was stressed. Of course, I was stressed. The doctor didn’t need to know it was because I was in a different city with a husband that can’t stop fighting with me, criticizing me, or using me for his own pleasures. That’s nothing the doctor could change or help me with. That was something I needed to visit a psychologist for, and I didn’t know if that would reduce my stress levels unless Jonathan changed.

Jonathan and I checked out of urgent care and headed for the parking lot. When we got out through the sliding glass doors of the urgent care unit, he kissed me on the forehead.

"I have to get back to work, hun. Go home and get some rest. I'll see you tonight."

That was the first time I had seen Jonathan since he disappeared when we left for Michigan for the weekend. I was at the point where I didn't care anymore. I headed home to rest. I couldn't help but think about what the doctor had said about stress. Could the stress of constantly fighting with Jonathan, the feeling that I am always walking on eggshells, or the feeling that I can never do anything right be what is affecting me physically?

That night after I had my shower and climbed into bed, Jonathan closed his book, flipped the sheets over his head, and slid down the bed, making his way to attempt to use his tongue and fingers to pleasure me. I wasn't in the mood, and I didn't want to make love. I flipped the comforter off him and said, "Not tonight, Jonathan. It's been a long day and I want to know why you aren't wearing your wedding ring."

Jonathan looked up at me, smiled, and then continued to try to fondle me without listening to my question. He completely ignored me. I got angry at his lack of respect toward me and my body.

"Are you kidding me right now?" I asked in amazement. Once again, he wanted to make love and was only thinking about himself.

"What's wrong with you now?" he suddenly snapped and changed moods. He became very irate that I was serious about saying "no" to him.

"Jonathan, I just want to sleep tonight."

"Okay, you can sleep once I have had my fun," he replied. He grabbed one of my breasts with force. He clearly didn't care about me or my health at all.

"Jonathan, let go," I said as I began to struggle free, trying to push his hand away, but he wouldn't let my breast go. "Jonathan, you're hurting me. Please stop!" I said, but he didn't let go.

For the first time in our marriage I was scared. I didn't think he would get abusive physically, but his violent sexual aggression toward me and the feeling that I might be raped by the man that I trusted was terrifying.

I couldn't break his grip from me, and he wasn't taking no for an answer. I was his to do with whatever he wanted and my helpless plea of "Stop, Jonathan" was met with, "You belong to me. This is my body, and I want it now. You have a duty as my wife. You will like it. Now spread them."

He continued to hold my breast with force with one hand, squeezing it hard enough that I felt a sharp pain with every squeeze, while trying vigorously to finger me with his other hand. None of this was a pleasure for me; it was like he was trying to give me pain on purpose to punish me for something I did wrong. Was this his way of disciplining me for going away for the weekend? By hurting me while he got his sick pleasures of being rough in bed like I enjoyed being in pain? Who was this man?

He had changed. He had become so aggressive and uncaring.

He had a different look about him. It was the look of an animal hunting their prey. It was cold and he was enjoying the power he was trying to assert over me. This was not the look of a husband's love toward his wife. It was one of enjoyment that he could inflict pain over me, and I was going to accept and even take pleasure from it.

"You want it rough? I will give it to you hard tonight.

You will know who your man is; you won't be able to walk when I am done with you," he said as he continued to molest me in an almost angry way.

I managed to kick his hand out, punch his chest, and free myself from his aggressive attack toward me. I jumped up from the bed, filled with fear and adrenalin. I didn't know what to think, but I knew I had said "No!" and he had full intentions on raping me. Like he had a full right to do whatever he pleased because he "owned" me. I was hysterical at this point.

Jonathan became outraged and punched the pillow beside my head.

"That's it, Kate, you are completely out of control and have lost your mind. We need to talk about our relationship now!" he snapped back with aggression. "We are having problems, and this isn't working for me!" he yelled, frustrated that he couldn't fuck me like he had every night for the past year, whether I wanted to or not.

"Jonathan, tonight is not the time for that conversation. I don't feel well. I had a draining day. I need sleep!" I yelled, completely emotional. I was shaking and I didn't know what to do, but I knew I couldn't be in the bedroom with him.

"You are losing it, Kate. You're going crazy! I may have to call CPS if you continue like this. I fear for the girls."

"I swear I will take you to court and take you for everything you have if you get my girls involved in your sick attempt to get to me."

At this point I was crying and angry and feeling like I needed to defend myself physically, verbally, and emotionally. All I wanted to do was pack my clothes and leave forever.

"Are you threatening me, Katelyn? Is that a threat?" he yelled back.

"No, it's not a threat," I replied with a quivering voice. "Just leave me alone. I am going to sleep on the couch."

I got up and headed for the couch. Jonathan didn't let me go. Instead, he put on his robe and followed behind me, yelling at me to come back. He was overly aggressive at that point and was determined to come after me.

"Katelyn, come back to our bedroom at once. You are being completely crazy!"

"No, Jonathan, I am just going to sleep here tonight," I replied as I laid a fleece blanket on top of me to cover up.

"If you don't get back to bed right now, the first call I make in the morning is going to be to a divorce lawyer, young lady. I wasn't done with you. Get back into our bed now."

"No," I replied.

"Kate, just come to bed. I will let you sleep tonight." His voice had changed. He went from aggressive and in a fighting mode to calm again. For the first time, I was scared to listen to him because of his erratic mood shift from his enraged and hostile behavior to suddenly calm and collected. I didn't want to wake the girls up. They didn't need to see what was going on or that I was sobbing and afraid. "Please," he said again. "I won't touch you."

I didn't reply; I didn't have the energy. I was afraid, tired, emotionally drained, and in pain from how he had been touching me. I didn't want to go, but since I didn't want to wake the girls, I got up off the couch and quietly headed to our bed to go back to sleep. I slept on my side with my back facing him so that he knew I wasn't going to talk or give him the chance to make any more advances. I didn't sleep the entire night. I was worried about what he would do next, and if he was just aggressive toward me sexually or if it would turn violent. For the first time, I was afraid for me and the girls after seeing how he could easily swing toward being violent and physical. Over the years he was abusive emotionally, verbally, and especially sexually, making me feel crazy and calling me names, but I was scared he would get violent.

The next morning, I made the decision that I could no longer be with a man that obviously masked his true colors and hid his personality from me.

This was not the man I dated; this was not the man I fell in love with. He was demeaning, condescending, hurtful, and controlling. I needed to get out of this life I once thought was a dream come true.

CHAPTER TWELVE
Perfect Doesn't Exist

THERE COMES A TIME IN ONE'S LIFE WHEN TRYING TO make something work is no longer an option. When walking away outweighs the ability to try harder. Looking back over my years of marriage, I have seen my health become compromised and my relationship turn so toxic that just the thought of going home gave me anxiety. I had nothing left to give to my marriage. I couldn't stand the fact that the man I had promised to love, honor, and cherish didn't apply the same vows back toward me. The man I wanted to spend the rest of my life with knew nothing about my life, didn't value me as an equal, and above all was abusive in so many ways. I had to keep my day-to-day activities to myself to avoid arguments. I now constantly walked on eggshells and was even to the point that I didn't want to share my life with him. I was always told I could be read like a book, but after being with Jonathan, I was different and the complete opposite. I learned how to be closed off–both emotionally and verbally. I didn't share my thoughts or my days, and I absolutely didn't tell him how I was feeling or else he'd undermine my opinions, or I'd get criticized for being too emotional. It became amazingly easy to withhold my day and thoughts from

Jonathan at the end of our marriage because he would come home late in the evening and would go straight to the den until 10 p.m. We would greet each other and that was only if we happened to cross paths. Then he would go to bed where he waited for our mechanical routine sex unless I was being punished for something and then he would shut the door to keep me out. Our relationship was no longer salvageable. I focused all my attention on the girls, not giving Jonathan any hint or idea of what my day looked like other than generic texts. My barrage of texts now had exponentially plummeted and I barely received a "good morning" text most days. I no longer told him when I needed to see a doctor or what I was doing that gave him any reason to question me. Virtually we were at a point where there was no more conversation between us, and we were living separate lives. I became almost a cold distant roommate toward him that had sex with him to keep him at bay. I was pretty much his legal hooker that cleaned and cooked. And when I say "hooker" it's because I was so over "us" that I couldn't enjoy our intimacy, so he stopped trying to pleasure me. He was pretty much just climbing on to orgasm, then rolling over and going to sleep. I tolerated it to keep the peace while I prepared my things to leave. I didn't want to add the silent treatments and insulting texts about how horrible I was to my stress of how I was going to survive when I left him. So instead I chose to continue the facade temporarily that I was okay when deep down I felt empty, lonely, afraid, and worthless. I didn't want to feel like this anymore, but I couldn't leave without a plan because I had the girls. I needed to make sure that when I left, I was gone for good. It took me some time to come to terms emotionally, but I woke up one morning ready to make my move. I secretly made copies of all our documents and sent our text fights to my email so that I could print them out if needed. Over the next six months I covertly stashed cash inside a sock in my sock drawer to hide it from Jonathan. I was fortunate to be able to save because Jonathan continued paying for all the expenses of the house since it was his home. I opened a checking account under my own name so he couldn't see what I was doing and left the joint one active so he wouldn't suspect anything different. I borrowed money from my mother who pulled it from her retirement fund so I could retain a lawyer at Dempsey Law Firm, which is where I began my story.

I entered the law firm as a different woman. I was now a woman who spent her day questioning everything and constantly feeling unhappy and alone. I sat in the lawyer's office realizing I was no longer an independent, strong woman. I was a woman who allowed herself to be controlled and mistreated. How could I accept such poor behavior for five years and give him the control to dismantle my self-esteem? I was finally going to rescue myself from my toxic marriage and go back to being me again. Even though I had no idea who that was anymore after so many years of never doing anything right and being controlled on so many levels, I could move on and rediscover myself. Mrs. Dempsey was very empathetic toward me as she sat at her desk listening to me tell my story.

"Don't worry, dear, I will get you through this," she said.

I asked her if I could move out if it got unbearable. I told her I didn't trust him after he once told me, "I need you, Kate. I think you have placed a spell on me. I can't breathe without you near me."

Mrs. Dempsey looked me straight in the eye and said, "Move out."

I retained Mrs. Dempsey that day. It was strange, but it was at that moment a huge weight lifted off my shoulders. I felt lighter and free. It was the strangest feeling because it was like the stress and tension that I was holding in my shoulders were no longer trapped and the realization that I was going to be free and on my own, regardless of how I was going to do it, was liberating. Before I went home, I pulled into the apartment complex close to the girls' school and signed a one-year lease. I wanted to be sure I could move on a whim. I knew Jonathan would act out, and I wanted to move out as fast as I could pack the girls' clothes. Jonathan was sitting at his desk in the den. I walked in and he looked up over his reading glasses to acknowledge me.

"We need to talk," I said, as I took a seat on the pullout couch. Jonathan stood up from his desk and sat next to me. I was trying desperately to hold back the tears so I could tell him what I needed. I sat on top of my hands to keep them from shaking, but I couldn't control my right leg as it thumped like a rumbling motor of a classic sports car.

"What do you need, Kate? I am busy working."

I knew he was lying and watching some type of porno because the bookcase glass behind him reflected the image of a woman having sex on his screen. I never understood his obsession with porn since we had sex every night, but I knew half the time that he was down here in his den it was to watch porn.

"Jonathan, I saw a lawyer today. I want a divorce," I blurted out.

Tears burst from me. I wasn't sure this time why I was crying other than I didn't like confrontation. I had had time to process what I was doing on the car ride home, and even though I felt relief, I was also sad that my second marriage, which I had worked so hard to keep alive, was over. Jonathan patted his knee.

"Come sit on my lap, babe. You will be fine. It will all be better in the morning," he said as he devalued my decision and held his hand out to bring me in. It was like what I was saying was nonsense and I needed to just be quiet and sit on his lap to make everything go away.

"Are you joking? Did you not hear what I just said? I am filing for divorce, Jonathan; I am not going to sit on your lap," I said. My eyebrows scrunched in and my eyes squinted as I gazed at his nonchalant demeanor. I was in utter amazement he was yet again trying to belittle my opinion. All these years, I was married to a man that never valued me as an equal. All these years he just saw me as a play toy; my opinion, my thoughts, my feelings never mattered. Jonathan was only using me so he could get what he needed from me while he slowly worked on shrinking my self-worth.

"I did hear you, but you're being crazy and overdramatic again. You just need a hug and some rest. You will be fine in the morning," he said, still not taking what I announced seriously.

I stood up, not even bothering to try to control my shaking hands as rage poured out. At this point I was furious that he wasn't taking anything I said of value.

"Jonathan, I am leaving you and I am not crazy. I am through with this marriage and with us!" I screamed at him, spun around, and stormed out of his den, slamming the door behind me while swearing. "You're a rat bastard. I wish I had never met you!" is all he heard as the door was slamming shut. The next day Jonathan came home and disappeared into the den as he did most nights for the last few years of our marriage. Only this time it was different. He came out about an hour later and asked me to join him to talk. I got the kids settled with dinner and decided to let him have his say with my decision. I followed him into the den to give him a chance to talk. I was cold and distant in my emotions. I needed to stand strong because he wasn't going to change my decision. I knew I needed to move on, and Jonathan was going to throw out whatever card he could to change my mind.

"I know what the problem is, Kate. I think I know how to fix it. You are mentally and physically exhausted and it's taking a toll on our relationship. Why don't you quit your job? You can stay home and be with the kids. You're working, running around with the kids, trying to do homework, shopping, cleaning. It is too much for you. I will let you quit and run the house and bills. I will even give you my whole paycheck to manage."

"Really? You're the same person that has never shown me your paycheck or even given me access to your personal bank account. You're just going to hand over your paycheck?"

"Yes, but with one exception. You need to start seeing a psychologist to see if they can help and I will now require you to do everything around the house including anything extra I need. I will now be supporting both of us so you will have to take on extra responsibilities and be at my beck and call."

Jonathan had in such a perfectly eloquent way summed up our problems in our marriage as being all my fault again. I was the one that was emotionally drained, and it was ruining our marriage. Not only did I have to seek a psychologist for mental help, but now I needed to do absolutely everything as a reward for quitting my job and staying with him. I was basically going to be at his beck and call, but somehow that was going to help with our marriage. Not to mention if I quit, I was 100 percent under his control of what I spent and what I did. I was in amazement that he wasn't taking any responsibility for any of his behavior toward me. He expected me to resolve all my issues that were ruining our marriage in therapy. There was no point arguing anymore; I was done fighting and I was no longer in love with him. I had zero interest in going to a psychologist because that wasn't going to change his narcissistic abuse.

"Jonathan, I heard your offer, and I respectfully decline. Actually, I feel so sorry for you," I said as I stood up to leave.

Jonathan raised his eyebrows and proceeded to give me a look of curiosity and disbelief that his narcissistic guilt tactics no longer influenced me.

"What is that supposed to mean?" he snarled.

As I turned to walk away, I stopped and turned my head back to look at him.

"I feel sorry for you because you will never feel love in your heart and soul, and for that, you will never truly be happy. You will somehow ruin every relationship that could have been good, and you will end up alone. I wish you all the best in life, but it will be a life without me. Goodbye, Jonathan." I turned my head back and walked out of the den. An overwhelming surge of feelings came over me: the feeling of grief that my marriage was over, the feeling of relief that I no longer would sustain his manipulation and emotional abuse any longer, and the feeling of doubt–not knowing if I was doing the right thing or how I was going to support myself and my girls on my own again. Despite all the conflicting feelings that rushed through me as I walked away from Jonathan, I knew I needed to be strong and embrace the uncertainty. There was no stopping now.

CHAPTER THIRTEEN
LETTING GO

OUR LIFE IS MADE UP OF SO MANY CHAPTERS. Each chapter represents a different journey we lived through. Some chapters will be happy, others will be filled with sorrow, and yet some you wish were never written at all or could just skip over completely. I can honestly say that my marriage was a chapter in my life that taught me some unbelievably valuable life lessons. I guess those chapters that you wished never happened are the lessons in life that are supposed to make you wiser and stronger. I will have a long healing process due to the emotional abuse over the years, but I did learn things from my relationship that I will take with me for the rest of my life. Lessons that I will use to prevent the same hurt again. The most important lesson is to never ignore my inner voice and always trust my gut. There were so many red flags at the beginning that I would make excuses for or think I was overreacting to.

After walking on eggshells for so many years during our marriage to avoid any possibility of an argument, as well as enduring mental, emotional, and sexual abuse, I was left broken and exhausted and ready to start over.

We walked away with nothing. But the truth is, even though I left all the materialistic stuff behind, I was walking away with my girls–who are my everything–and my dignity. I was emotionally broken–hell, I was broken on so many levels–but I knew it was temporary; I would heal myself over time, and I would go on living my life. So, in the end, what I know to be true is if I had the strength to leave, I would eventually recover and would survive.

ABOUT ISABEL WELLS

Natasha Barber is a published children's book author who writes under the name Isabel Wells for her novels. She is an award-winning Autism Advocate and founder of the non-profit Autism Moms Know Safety. She has appeared on *Autism Live*, and her articles have been featured in *Autism Parenting Magazine*. She is the recognized author of the Tommy's Lessons children's book series. Books in the series include *My Tomato, Guacamole, and Onion Sandwich*; *My Magic Pet Fish*; *My Super Cool Ant Farm*; and *My Super Slimy Fish Bait*; as well as the Autism children's book, *The Waiting Song*, published by Future Horizons. Her passion and inspiration are her boys.

See more on her author website:
www.NatashaBarber.org.
www.Isabel-Wells.com

EMOTIONALLY BROKEN

Katelyn was a blue-collar single mother working in one of Detroit's steel mills, trying to keep up with everything life kept throwing at her. Katelyn kept to herself socially, not making any time for going out on the town or dating. During the company's continuous improvement efforts, Jonathan–a successful senior manager from Chicago–was brought in.

Jonathan was handsome, charming, and turned Katelyn's world upside down. She found herself daydreaming and thinking naughty thoughts about him all day, every day. Jonathan was her knight in shining armor, sweeping her off her feet and saying vows to love, honor, and cherish her during a romantic getaway.

Katelyn's fairy-tale marriage ended with shattered vows of control, criticism, and narcissistic abuse, but she was strong and would not confine herself to her circumstances. Letting go of the toxic relationship–with her two girls and her dignity–was all she could do.

www.ingramcontent.com/pod-product-compliance
Lightning Source LLC
LaVergne TN
LVHW050642100826
845148LV00011B/1950

* 9 7 8 0 5 7 8 7 1 4 9 6 7 *